"*I know who it is. . . .*"

"I know who it is," she announces.

"You know who what is?"

"Well," she begins. Her eyebrows arch, and she's back into cool.

Riddles again? I'm not in the mood. "Just go ahead and tell me, okay?"

"I know who gave Connie Tibbs AIDS." There's a silence. "Aren't you going to ask who?"

"No."

"Well, I'll tell you anyway. It's — "

"Stop!"

"What?"

"I don't want to know."

Rae's cheeks puff with displeasure. "Come off it, Karen. This is deep."

"I don't care, Rae. It's not just deep. It's about a person. A girl our age. And she's sick. Really, really sick."

Other Point paperbacks
you will enjoy:

Sheila's Dying
by Alden Carter

Storm Rising
by Marilyn Singer

Life Without Friends
by Ellen Emerson White

I Can Hear the Mourning Dove
by James Bennett

Until Whatever

MARTHA HUMPHREYS

SCHOLASTIC INC.
New York Toronto London Auckland Sydney

No part of this publication may be reproduced in whole or in part, or stored in a retrieval system, or transmitted in any form or by any means, electronic, mechanical, photocopying, recording, or otherwise, without written permission of the publisher. For information regarding permission, write to Clarion Books, an imprint of Houghton Mifflin Company, 215 Park Avenue South, New York, NY 10003.

ISBN 0-590-46616-X

12 11 10 9 8 7 6 5 4 3 2 1   3 4 5 6 7 8/9

Printed in the U.S.A.   01

First Scholastic printing, May 1993

Until
Whatever

chapter one

↪ It's Wednesday, the second day of school. I've stopped by my locker to pick up a book for first-period class. Across the hall a group of kids I usually hang around with are laughing and talking.

"Karen!" Rae Scudder breaks away from the group and darts up to me. Her face is flushed, her dark hair tousled. "Have you heard?" she gasps.

"Heard what?"

"Karen, everyone's talking about it."

I sigh. Rae has this habit of turning every bit of news, every conversation, into some big, suspenseful thing.

"At least," she goes on, "all our friends are talking about it."

And they're the ones who matter, I think. That's what would be in Rae's mind; she is a bit of a snob. "Just tell me what it is." More resigned than curious, I shut my locker.

"Connie Tibbs has AIDS."

My head jerks up as a memory surfaces. An April day. The river. Connie Tibbs standing on the river-bank. I stare at Rae as if she's grown horns.

"Well," Rae says, "she does."

"Okay." I won't argue the fact, but my mind reels—from more than memories. Connie Tibbs and AIDS? The two things don't go together. Gays have AIDS. Addicts who share needles in aban-doned buildings have AIDS. But Connie? She can't have AIDS. She's this really terrific-looking blonde, always smiling, always happy.

"Come on, Karen." Rae sounds impatient, and I wonder if she's angry that I'm not immediately tearing into this piece of gossip. "You do know who Connie is, don't you?" she presses.

"Of course."

"Well, I can just imagine what she did to get it." Rae's mouth prisses. "Those friends of hers are horrible."

I shrug. Connie's friends aren't horrible. Sure they dress tough and no one dares to pick a fight with them, but it's not like they're some gang riding around on motorcycles and terrorizing people.

Rae, of course, continues talking, getting more and more involved with her news. "It was probably that Bobby Hensen. Everyone knows he and Con-nie—"

A bell rings, and kids, still milling about in the hallway, switch into purposeful action. Locker close. Groups of girls split into pairs or trios and head for class. Guys slap hands and part with grunted words or phrases.

"Later, man."

"Football field at four."

Rae glances at her watch. "I gotta run. My first class is way over in Building D. But at lunch I'll tell you everything I know." She takes off.

"Rae," I call, "I'm not . . ." Too late. She's gone— around a corner and out of sight. "I'm not sure I want to hear everything you know," I mutter to myself. All in all, as I move on from being stunned, I decide the news about Connie is pretty sad.

Of course at lunch I do hear about it. Rae, her dark eyes gleaming, tells me. Between bites of spaghetti and salad and bread and finally cherry pie, she talks.

"Ruth James's mother works in Dr. Springarden's office and this is what Ruth told me. Connie had this cold. One of those sore throat, coughy things. And it wouldn't go away; it just kept getting worse. So her mother made her go for a checkup. Dr. Springarden started it, but I think they finally had to put her in the hospital overnight. Yeah. They did. 'Cause that's how they found out she had it. They put her in, did a whole bunch of other tests, and found out she was positive. Or the rabbit died." Rae stops and waits.

I guess I'm supposed to laugh, but I don't. I just stare at her.

She puffs an impatient breath. "Karen, that was a joke. You know, like when someone's pregnant?"

Again I refuse to respond.

"Okay," she goes on, "forget it. Anyway, she has it. Mrs. James didn't find out how she got it, but you know what that whole crowd is like. I figure Connie was messing around with some guy who'd . . . you know. Been with other guys. Or maybe some guy who was doing drugs. Ruth says Connie was probably shooting up herself, but I don't think so. I know kids who've had classes with her, and they never said she was spacy or weird. Just wild. She talks a lot about sex, and all sorts of guys hang around, just waiting to walk her from class to class. And I know for a fact that she slept with Gary Denison."

"Do you?" I interrupt. Rae's really taking this too far. "You know for a fact that Connie slept with someone? You were there?"

"No, but Amy Harper, that real brainy kid who sings in the choir at my church, told me. Holy cow! All those guys Connie slept with? They'll have to be tested. And some of them probably have it. They'll kill her. That is, if she hasn't killed them first."

Another joke? I wonder. I sip some milk.

"They'll kill her? Unless she . . . Come on, Karen. Do I have to explain everything?"

"No."

"And—Oh! There's already some parents' group forming that doesn't want her to go to school here.

They say she's putting us all at risk. Personally I don't know if she is or not. So I'm not sure they should put her out. I mean, after all, she is sick. But then I'm not really involved. I don't have any classes with her, and we've never been friends, so we're not about to do anything intimate. But if I saw her coming out of the bathroom? I don't know. I think I'd think twice about going in. What about you? What do you think?"

"I think Ruth's mother should have kept her mouth shut."

"Oh, Karen! Lighten up." Rae glares at me, and lunch ends on a pretty sour note.

And now I'm in Biology. Class hasn't started yet, so I'm sitting here, thumbing through my text and wondering when we'll have to do horrible things to a dead frog. I realize everyone's awfully quiet and look up, figuring the teacher has come in. But he hasn't. So why the silence? I glance around. Books are open. Kids are reading, some of them even jotting down notes. Or maybe they're just doodling. Anyway, they're applying pencil to paper, and that, on the second day of school with no teacher in the room, is strange.

I notice that occasionally someone glances toward the back of the room. I turn, and there, seated alone at a table, is Connie Tibbs. Did I see her yesterday and not recognize her? Possibly. The blond hair, usually billowing out like a movie star's, is pulled back, held away from her face by a scarf. There's less makeup than I remember. And does she already look thinner, or is that just my imagination?

"Good afternoon." Mr. Boggs strides into the room, his textbook and a manila folder tucked in his right hand. He's tall and thin and new, so none of us knows what to expect. "Have you had a chance to look at your text?" he asks.

Like everyone else, I nod.

"Any questions on it? Or the course description we went over in class yesterday?"

I want to ask if we're really going to slice up frogs, but I don't. I've learned that it's best not to attract a teacher's attention too early in the year.

"Hey, Mr. Boggs." Brian Mahoney, a boy seated off to my right, waves his hand. "There's a chapter on sex and stuff. Are we gonna cover that?"

"Wasn't it on the schedule?"

"Yeah." Brian grins. "But what about the stuff you can get from sex? VD? Herpes? Other things?" He sneers when he says "other things" and glances around the room.

The class begins to stir, and I'm pretty sure what everyone's thinking about. Even in a large suburban high school, news about someone having AIDS travels fast.

"Enough!" Mr. Boggs raps on his desk with a ruler. "We'll cover those subjects, and if you want to ask questions, you may do so. But only when the time comes and then in an orderly and well-mannered fashion."

"Orderly and well-mannered?" the boy next to me mutters. "Where does he think he is? Some prep school?"

"But first"—Mr. Boggs opens his manila folder and stares down at it—"this is a large class, and I'll need help getting to know who you are. I've worked out a seating chart that—"

"A seating chart?" The first murmur comes from the back of the room. Others follow.

"Oh, no!"

"You think we're third graders?"

"Class!" Again Mr. Boggs brings his ruler down on the desk. "I'll remind you once—and only once—that I'm in charge. That means my word is law. If I say we sit according to a seating chart, that's the way we sit. If I say that on some days we get out of class five minutes early, that's what will happen. And if I say that disruptions mean that everyone loses five points on the first major test, that will also happen. Is that understood?"

Lloyd Caruthers, one of the school's wise guys, shoots his hand up in the air. "Does that mean you don't grade on the curve?"

"I grade," Mr. Boggs says, "on how well you do. But let me warn you. How well you do isn't just tests and homework. How well you do also includes classroom behavior."

The class quiets down, and I know Mr. Boggs has won his first battle. We suburban kids may be an unruly lot at times, but most of us are college bound. Hitting us in the grades hurts.

Mr. Boggs scans the room and nods. "Now let's get on with business." He removes his seating chart from the manila folder.

Soon everything's a big jumble. We're all over the classroom—a few of us in seats, most not. Someone's name is called; he's assigned to a table. The person sitting at that table gets up, stands by the wall, and waits for his own name to be called. I resign myself to a pretty long wait. I've been sitting in the second row of tables, and my last name is Thompson. So I perch on one of the bookcases that line the room under the windows and wait.

Garrett. Lancaster. Lucas. Nesbit. Mr. Boggs drones on. Finally there are only five of us standing: me, Connie, and three guys.

Then it happens. Connie and I are assigned to the same table. I should have figured we would be. Thompson? Tibbs? What else?

We sit down. I look over at her and smile. She smiles back. Tentatively. Like someone who's been kicked in the teeth a few times and doesn't know what to expect next.

"Hey, Karen." Clyde Wilson, one of the last three boys to be assigned to tables, pauses beside me on his way to the back of the room. "Just don't take any deep breaths. Maybe then you'll be okay."

Connie's smile fades. Her face is masklike, expressionless, as she stares up at Mr. Boggs. He begins the day's lecture.

"Clyde's a jerk," I whisper. But Connie ignores me.

In fact, she continues to ignore me until the class is over. Then, gathering up her books, focusing totally on those books, she says, "I'm sure Mr. Boggs will change your seat if you ask him. All you have to do is explain why."

"Connie, I—"

"And if you're feeling some sort of obligation because of that business"—with an airy gesture, she dismisses the short time many years ago when we were friends—"forget it."

"What if I—"

"Besides, there's an uneven number of students in here. Everyone will be much happier if I work by myself." She sweeps away. Her head is high, her shoulders ramrod straight as she sails out into the hallway. Her posture gives me a jolt. She's proud. She's not about to take anything from anyone. How long, I wonder, will she be able to stay that way?

For a minute or two I sit there and think about what she's said. I could forget that she and I once were friends. Our lives haven't touched since then. We've hung around with different kids. Even our classes have been different. I've been on the college track, taking stuff like Biology, Algebra, and German. Connie takes classes for kids who plan on getting jobs right after they graduate. Typing. Shorthand. So why should I get mixed up with her now? Shoot. She probably shouldn't even be in this class. Perhaps her being here is some sort of administrative error. If so, it'll be easy enough to get a new lab partner. I glance toward the front of the room, where Mr. Boggs is busy explaining something to a student. Okay. My problem can wait. If I do decide I want a new lab partner, I can ask him about it later.

I gather up my books. I have one more class to go, and the second day of school will be over.

An hour and a half later I'm outside, scanning the parking lot. Todd, my boyfriend, is supposed to drive me home, but he's late. So I'm standing here at the top of three flights of cement steps, wilting in the muggy September heat and wondering why this morning it seemed like such a great idea to bring a sweater.

"Karen?"

I look around, and it's Rae. She's grinning from ear to ear.

"I know who it is," she announces.

"You know who what is?"

"Well," she begins. Her eyebrows arch, and she's back into cool.

Riddles again? I'm not in the mood. "Just go ahead and tell me, okay?"

"I know who gave Connie Tibbs AIDS." There's a silence. "Aren't you going to ask who?"

"No."

"Well, I'll tell you anyway. It's—"

"Stop!"

"What?"

"I don't want to know."

Rae's cheeks puff with displeasure. "Come off it, Karen. This is deep."

"I don't care, Rae. It's not just deep. It's about a person. A girl our age. And she's sick. Really, really sick."

"Yeah, but it's not like she's cool or anything. She's done all sorts of things."

I turn away.

Rae goes on. "That's how you get this disease. At least that's what they tell us. You—"

I stop listening, and pretty soon I realize Rae has stopped talking. She's staring at me kind of thoughtful like.

"You gonna tell me what's going on?" she asks.

I shrug. Rae and I are friends. Why shouldn't I tell her? "Connie and I kind of hung around together for a while."

"I didn't know that."

"It was before you moved to town."

"The dark ages, huh?"

"Yeah," I say with almost a smile. "Back when my parents were getting their divorce."

"Oh."

Rae knows all about my parents' divorce. Just like I know that one of her brothers flunked out of college. See? Sometimes we really can talk. Maybe this will be one of those times.

I perch on a stone wall and feel a blast of warm air ruffle my hair. "I guess it started the day my dad left."

"It?"

"My friendship with Connie." Actually I know it started that day. I remember everything about that day. I'd come home from school. My mother was sitting in the living room, her eyes red, her mouth a thin, stern line. "My mother told me Dad was gone, and I raced out of the house. I didn't wait for explanations or anything. I just started running. I wound up at the river, sort of north of town. And then, I don't know why I did it, but I just walked on in."

"The water?" Rae asks.

"Yeah."

"With your clothes on?"

I hear the amusement in Rae's voice and sense an attitude. Maybe this isn't going to be one of our landmark conversations. Or maybe it is. For all the wrong reasons. "It was April. You know it's still pretty cold in April."

"So you left your clothes on to go swimming in the river. Because it was cold."

"Oh, Rae."

"And you met Connie there? In the river? Both of you swimming around with your clothes on?"

I won't let Rae get to me. "I got caught by one of those undercurrents. When I came to, I was on the riverbank. Connie was sitting beside me."

Rae hums softly.

I recognize the tune—a real golden oldie, "Jim Dandy to the Rescue." That does it. I have nothing else to say to her. I stand up and start down the first flight of stairs.

Rae comes after me. "Okay. I'm sorry. She saved your life and the two of you became really tight."

"We became friends," I say grudgingly.

"And now you feel you have to be her friend again. Regardless of who her friends are. Regardless of who *your* friends are."

"I don't know." Like it or not, Rae is getting to me. "Maybe I just feel we shouldn't dump on her because she's had some bad luck."

"Some bad luck? Karen, she's a walking time bomb. An accident waiting to happen. An—"

A car honks. I look into the parking lot and see that it's Todd. A sense of relief sweeps over me. "I gotta go. See you later."

"Karen," Rae calls, "we haven't finished this. We—"

I wave her silent and continue down the steps and across the parking lot to Todd and Clara Car. Clara Car? Yes, his car is named, a name picked out by Todd himself. She's this 1958 pink Pontiac, and—I sometimes think—the real love of his life.

"Hi," I say as I open Clara's door and climb in. "Boy, did you show up at the right time."

"Oh?"

"I was getting stuck in this conversation with Rae."

Todd grins; we both know what Rae can be like. I start to relax. Gee, I like being with him. I like just sitting here and looking at him. Wavy blond hair. Brown eyes. A spattering of freckles that he claims he'll outgrow. I don't know. They were there when he was eight. Ten years have passed, and they still haven't shown signs of fading, let alone going away.

He shifts gears and pulls out of the parking lot. "I hear a conversation with Rae isn't all you got stuck in today."

"Oh?"

"I was talking to Brian Mahoney. He says you wound up with Connie Tibbs as your lab partner."

"I did." I slump down in the seat. Does everyone know about Connie Tibbs? And if they know about her, do they have to talk about her? It's a conversation I've had enough of and sure would like to avoid now. I look out the window at clusters of kids leaving school on foot.

"Boy," I say, "it's so easy to pick out the freshmen."

"It is?" Todd doesn't sound all that interested, but then he's in the left lane, waiting for a chance to make a really nasty turn.

"Yeah. Look."

He glances to his right, where three girls walk with their heads bent forward. They giggle; they whisper things to each other. A fourth watches wistfully as Todd and I creep forward in the left-turn lane.

"I used to be like that," I say.

"Like what?"

"Envious of upperclassmen with boyfriends. Wondering if I'd ever start to date."

"But you did."

"Yeah." Two years ago Todd and I stopped being just friends; we became an item. And since then it's been great. A date every Saturday night. An escort for all the big dances. A weeknight study partner.

Todd makes his left turn. "So," he says, "what are you going to do about it?"

"About what?"

"Having Connie as a lab partner."

So much for the conversation I'd like to avoid. "I don't know. Probably nothing."

"Nothing," he echoes. "You mean you're not gonna have the teacher get you another partner?"

"Isn't one enough?" Will humor save the day? Or at least the ride home? I look at Todd's glowering expression. Scratch humor.

"I'm serious," he says.

"So am I. Connie and I were assigned to be lab partners, and I'll stick with it." I hear myself and wonder when I actually made that decision. When Connie said I didn't owe her anything? When Mr. Boggs was busy with another student? Perhaps when I told Rae about Connie saving my life.

Todd stops for a traffic light. "I bet if you asked, you could get a new lab partner without even giving the teacher a reason. Brian says he's a real weenie."

"He's not." I remember Brian mouthing off about the stuff you could get from sex. I also remember how well Mr. Boggs handled the situation.

"Okay then, maybe you'll have to tell him the whole story."

"I'm not going to."

"Why not?" Todd turns onto Grover Street.

"Maybe I think too many people already know about Connie." My house is only three blocks away, and I'm looking forward to getting there. Today I probably won't even ask Todd in.

"But you're not gonna work with her, are you?"

"Sure I am." My resolve is getting stronger. Also my annoyance at having to talk about the subject at all. "It's not any big deal."

"Suppose you get sick," Todd presses.

"I won't get sick. You don't catch AIDS by sitting at the same table with someone." I wish I felt as sure about that as I sounded.

"But you won't just be sitting there. This is Biology we're talking about. You'll be dissecting things.

Using knives. Suppose you both cut yourselves at the same time."

"Suppose we do. You think we'll touch fingers and become blood sisters?"

"Not on purpose, but some sort of accident could happen."

"Then I'll stick my finger in formaldehyde. Doesn't that kill everything?"

"You know it doesn't. Particularly not something like AIDS."

"I was kidding."

"Come on, Karen." Todd frowns; clearly he's displeased. "You could at least take this seriously."

"And you could lighten up."

Todd's lips tighten into a thin line, making him look just about as angry as I feel.

A few seconds later, when he doesn't show any sign of relaxing, I inch away from him. Bunched up next to the door, I watch houses go past. Medium-size houses with tidy front lawns. Driveways leading to carports or garages. A nice, comfortable neighborhood.

Still silent, Todd drives the rest of the way to my house, stops in front, and cuts off the motor.

"I don't think you better come in today," I say, climbing out of the car. "I've got tons of homework."

"Yeah?" Todd says. "Well, that's okay. I've got stuff to do, too." He drives off.

I let myself into the house.

"That you?" my mother calls from the kitchen.

No, it's the Loch Ness monster arriving home right on schedule, three-thirty every afternoon. "Yeah, it's me. But what are you doing here?" My mother is part owner of a dress shop in the mall. Finding her home this early in the afternoon is pretty weird.

"Not much business," she says, "so I left Mavis in charge. What about you? Nice day at school?"

"Sure." Except for finding out that Connie Tibbs has AIDS. Except for arguing with my two closest friends. "Real nice day." And I don't want to say any more about it.

chapter two

I'm already sitting at our table when Connie enters Biology the next day. She's surprised to see me there. She tries to hide it, but I can tell. Her eyes widen the tiniest fraction of an inch; there's a break in her stride as she starts down the center aisle. She sits beside me.

"Hi," I say.

"What are you doing here?" she asks.

"This is my assigned seat, remember?"

"I don't need you to feel sorry for me." She sets her books on the table and loops the shoulder strap of her purse over the back of the chair.

"I don't feel sorry for you."

"And I don't want you to think—"

"Hey!" I raise my hands. "I don't think. I'm a student. A teacher tells me to sit somewhere, I sit."

"But . . . Oh, never mind." Connie shrugs, a gesture that dismisses me.

"Time to get started." Mr. Boggs enters just as the bell rings. He draws a squiggly circle on the blackboard, pulls some index cards out of a pocket, points at the board, and says, "That is a cell." And for the next twenty minutes we hear about cells— what they do, what they contain. Finally he puts down his cards and announces that for the rest of the period we will have our first in-class lab.

I hear a few moans; I see some grimaces.

"It's not the frog, is it?" one of the grimacers calls out.

"No," Mr. Boggs says, "the frog comes later. Wilson! Willoughby!"

Two boys who had been whispering to each other look up.

"If you two can control your adolescent need to gossip, I could use volunteers to pass out slides and microscopes."

Mr. Boggs writes on the board, and the class, released from the need to pay attention, begins to whisper. I glance at Connie. She stares straight ahead, making no sign that she wants to talk. I fold my hands on the table and wait.

Pretty soon Clyde Wilson places a microscope on our table. "Hey, Karen," he says, "just make sure you go first. After she uses the stuff, it'll have to be destroyed."

"Oh, Clyde," I snarl, "grow up!"

But he's at the next table, giggling and pointing back at Connie.

So Connie and I sit there in an embarrassed silence. Finally she says, "Well? Do you want to go first?"

"Not particularly."

She stands—managing somehow to make the change in position a statement of defiance—and peers into the microscope. "Your turn," she says minutes later as she sits back down.

I'm leaning down to look through the microscope when a thought, perhaps brought on by Clyde's nasty comment, strikes me. Bodily fluids, I think. That's how everyone says AIDS is transmitted. Are tears bodily fluids? Suppose when Connie looked into the microscope, she bent real close, and her eye had . . . ? Shoot. I'm being silly. She wasn't crying into the microscope; she was looking through it. And so I force myself to look.

She's staring at me when I sit back down. "What's the matter?" she asks. "Scared I contaminated something?"

"No." All right. So I'm lying. Sue me.

"Took you an awful long time to get down to that microscope."

"I was wondering exactly what we were supposed to look for."

"I think we're about to find out." She nods toward the front of the room.

Mr. Boggs has written specific instructions on the board and goes over them with us. Connie and I look through the microscope again. This time I will myself not to be scared, and it pretty much works.

"Did you see everything?" I ask when we're finished.

"I think so." She's adding a sentence to her notes.

"The nucleus?"

"Yeah. If that's the part that looks like an egg yolk."

"It is," I say. "What about cytoplasm?"

"That's the stuff outside the nucleus, I think."

I check my notes. "Me too. And the nuclear membrane?"

"The wall, that line, around the nucleus."

"I guess we did okay." I toss my pencil down on the table and lean back in my chair. "And it wasn't even too bad."

"I don't think it gets bad until later."

"Not until . . . " I pause and make a big production out of what comes next. "The frog," I say dramatically.

Connie laughs. It's that warm, full-bodied laugh I remember from the short time we were friends, and I'm glad to hear it again.

"You know," she says, "it's not always a frog."

"It's not? What is it?"

"A friend of mine who goes to another school had to cut up a cat."

"A cat!" I shudder. "All that fur? Ugh!"

"I think it's skinned before you start."

"Doesn't matter. There's no way I could cut open a cat." I look at Connie, she looks at me, and we both realize: We're talking, we're laughing. We're two ordinary kids, starting a year of working together. And maybe picking up on a friendship that began and ended a whole lot of years ago.

"Hey, Connie," I say, "it's gonna be okay."

Rae catches up with me after school. I've put most of my books in my locker and am heading toward the main entrance. "Where were you at lunch?" she asks. "Todd and I saved you a place."

"I had a phone call to make."

"You still had to eat."

"I had a sandwich outside."

She falls into step beside me. "Your loss. I have really great news, and you could have found out about it three hours earlier."

"What is it?" I force myself to ask. Truth is, I'm not all that eager to hear. Recently Rae's news flashes have been less than good.

"That group I told you about? The one that's gonna get Connie Tibbs kicked out of school?"

"Yeah."

"They're meeting Saturday morning at ten. Here. In the gymnasium."

"And I should think that's great news? Even after what I told you yesterday afternoon?" I step outside, skirting a group of students clustered near the entrance.

Rae's still close on my heels. "Oh, Karen. Sometimes you're so dense. They'll meet, Connie'll get her walking papers, and you won't have to worry about some silly sense of loyalty."

"I'm not worried." I head down the front steps and turn left.

"Hey, eraser brain," Rae says, "the parking lot's that way." She points to her right.

"I know."

"Then where are you going?"

"Downtown. I have an appointment."

"Oh?" She stands there, her head tipped to one side as she waits for details.

But I don't give her any. I wave and hurry across the street to a bus stop. Actually, I admit to myself, it's kind of fun to leave her there, looking all flustered and annoyed.

Of course, what with the appointment and all, I'm late getting home.

"Mom?" I call as I enter the house. I glance first in the living room, then in the dining room. The table, I notice, is set for dinner. "Mom?"

My mother comes in from the kitchen. "Karen," she begins. Above her glasses, her forehead crinkles into a frown. "Do you realize it's after six?"

"No. Well, yes." No point in starting out with a lie.

"I was so worried."

"I know. But the . . . " I stop. It's too soon. I'll have to tell my mother where I was, but the second I enter the house? No way.

My mother, though, is not listening. "Traffic gets so heavy. The nearest bus stop is three blocks away. And crime. Even in the best neighborhoods, it—"

"Mom, I'm all right. It's just that this afternoon . . . well, things took longer . . . " I give up. "Let me . . . A minute." Needing to pull myself together, I gesture with my books and purse, then dart back out of the dining room. The past hour, talking to our family doctor about Connie, about AIDS, has been a real downer. I put my stuff on the foyer table and catch a glimpse of myself in the hall mirror. My eyes are clear. My color's good. But suppose it wasn't? Suppose I was sick. Suppose I had . . . ? Suppose I was going to . . . ? No. The whole idea is too depressing.

I go back into the dining room, where my mother now has dinner on the table. She's serving up some sort of casserole. I slip into my seat; she hands me my plate.

"Karen," she says, "I want to know where you were."

It's her brook-no-nonsense tone, so I know that as much as I may want to delay, I can't. I take a breath. "I had an appointment."

"At school?"

"With Dr. Patterson."

"Dr. Patterson?" Alarm springs into my mother's gray eyes. I knew she was going to panic; I didn't want her to panic. "Our Dr. Patterson?" she presses.

"Yes, but nothing's wrong."

"Then why . . . " Her eyes widen. "Is it Todd? Karen, are you and Todd—"

"No!" I break in quickly. I know what she's about to ask, and I'm embarrassed. Forget those books about families and open communication. What I've found is that whenever my mother and I get anywhere near the subject of sex, things get weird.

"Because," she continues, "I want you to know that if anything does happen, you can always—"

"Mom! Everything's okay. Really."

"Then why did you see Dr. Patterson?" she asks.

"It's no big deal," I say, hoping I can convince her of that. "It's just that there's this girl in school with AIDS."

"AIDS?"

"I wanted some information."

There's a silence while my mother butters a roll. My guess is she's trying to get a handle on the conversation. "I doubt you really needed information," she finally says. "Pine Bluff is a large school. One person with AIDS? That doesn't mean you'll be having any real contact with that person."

"Well, I sort of wound up in a class with her."

"A class?"

"She's my Bio partner."

"Your Bio partner?"

I don't think my mother realizes she's doing this parrot thing. I think she's genuinely concerned.

"Fourth period," I say. "Mr. Boggs's class. He's new."

"A lab?"

I nod.

"Oh, Karen, you'll be working with her so closely. Suppose—"

"It's okay, Mom. I asked Dr. Patterson about all that. He said the only way I could get AIDS from her would be through an exchange of bodily fluids. You know. Like blood. Or sex."

"You could cut yourselves. You could—"

"Mom! All Dr. Patterson said was that I should be careful."

"Will you be?"

"Of course." My mother looks doubtful, so I go on. "Look, Dr. Patterson didn't think it was all that big a deal. He said there was just one thing I absolutely shouldn't let happen."

"What's that?"

"He said I shouldn't let my lab partner bite me." Again, as it had in Dr. Patterson's office, an image of Connie nipping at my heels appears. It amuses me still, and I smile.

"Karen, I don't think this is funny."

"It's not funny." And I'm no longer smiling. "It's just that it's . . ."

"It seems to me, Karen, that the solution is pretty simple." The worried edge has vanished from my mother's voice; she's back in control now. Ice tinkles as she stirs sugar into her tea. "You'll talk to your teacher. Explain the problem. I'm sure he'll assign you a new—"

"No!" I've had this new-lab-partner conversation before, and I'm not going through it again.

My mother's eyebrows knit in a frown. She pushes her glasses up on the bridge of her nose. "Is there something else going on here? Karen, do you know this person?"

I wait a moment before answering. "It's Connie Tibbs."

"Tibbs." My mother searches her memory. "Wasn't she the girl you were friends with right after your father left?"

"Yes."

"Oh, my. Karen!" It's obvious that details are coming back to her. "That house over in Mill Village. That brother."

"Oh, Mom." My mother, the snob. All my life she's tried to convince me that addresses and families were important. All my life I've resisted believing her. We used to argue about it. But now, since we've both grown up, there's this unspoken truce. At least most of the time.

"Wasn't he arrested, Karen? Robbery or something? That old five-and-dime out on—"

"Mom! That was a long time ago. He must be grown up now. And I don't know where they live anymore. Things could be really different."

"In one way they certainly are." My mother's voice goes soft. "Now Connie has AIDS."

I look down and start pushing food around on my plate. There doesn't seem to be anything else to say. I know my mother's worried, but I don't want her to worry. I'm sixteen years old. I can take care of myself.

chapter three

It's Saturday morning, and I've made a decision. I'm going to that meeting Rae told me about, the one where they'll decide whether Connie can stay in school or not. I get up early, grab a piece of toast for breakfast, and leave. My mother's already out—probably at the shop. A lot of people buy clothes on Saturdays.

The walk to school is great. The sky is blue, the air a bit crisp. Leaves have just begun to turn color and fall. I scrunch through smatterings of them on the sidewalk whenever I can. It's a super morning, and I feel really good.

At school, though, all that changes. From the moment I enter the gymnasium, I don't like what I see. Adults mill about, most of them looking angry and mean. Groups form, and conversations turn into arguments. Gestures are sharp, impatient. My sense of happiness fades, and I wander around, searching for anyone I might know. Am I the only person under thirty attending?

Finally I find another student—Mike Rowen, this really strange guy who writes for the school newspaper. He's wearing what to him is a uniform—blue jeans, a sweatshirt that's too baggy to be fashionable, and dirty sneakers. His hair, which borders on red, sticks out at various angles because he's always running a hand through it or pulling at it. I hesitate for a minute, then go up to him.

"What do you make of all this?" I ask.

"It's a witch-hunt," he says. "The start of Dachau."

"Huh?" Almost immediately I regret deciding to talk to him. He's always making these offbeat historical or literary references. No one ever knows what he's talking about, so he takes great pleasure in explaining. That way he can show off how smart he is.

"Dachau," he says. "World War II? One of the concentration camps?"

"Oh." I'm not impressed.

"Anyway," he goes on, "the tribe has convened. They've found a member they can sacrifice. Maybe then the gods won't send any more disease, death, or famine their way."

"Gee," I say. "And I thought they were making the world safe for democracy."

"What?" It's Mike's turn to look puzzled.

"It's a quotation. Woodrow Wilson, explaining about World War I." I toss the line back over my shoulder as I start to walk away. There. I can play the reference game just as well as Mike.

Off to my right a voice booms, "Is that what you think?"

Alarmed by the angry tone, I turn.

A man grabs another man by the shirt lapels and pulls him up so that he's inches away from his face. "You'd think different if your kid had a class with that . . . that trash!"

"Gerry, please." A woman—his wife?—puts a hand on his arm and leads him away.

The second man straightens his shirt collar and joins a group of three men standing near him. "Did you see that?" he sputters. "Some clown manhandled me. Just let him come near me again. I'll make this a meeting he remembers."

"Wow," I whisper. "Didn't anyone levelheaded come to this meeting?"

"Meetings like this don't attract levelheaded people."

"You're here."

"I'm covering it for the paper." He grins. "You want to cover it, too?"

I shoot him a look. A couple of years back Mike and I were in this English class together where the teacher made us read our essays aloud. Since then he's been after me to write for the paper. But I've always been busy. With Rae. With Todd. With cheerleading. So now it's become a running joke.

Mike asks. He knows I'll say no, and I do. Of course, one of these days I might surprise him and say yes. But not today. I open my mouth, ready to respond.

"Your attention! May I have your attention, please?" Mr. Carlisle, our principal, stands behind a podium on a makeshift stage that's been set up under one of the basketball hoops. "Will everyone please be seated."

For a moment there, kidding around with Mike, I felt almost lighthearted. Now, though, Mr. Carlisle's businesslike tone brings me back into focus. The angry parents. The hostility radiating from so many conversations.

"Maybe getting started will make things calmer," I mutter, perching on the first row of the bleachers.

"I doubt it." Mike sits beside me. "He'd do better to feed the multitudes. Maybe throw out some raw meat. They might go for that instead of human flesh."

I watch as people file into the rows of folding chairs that have been placed on the basketball court. No one sits very close to anyone else; no one looks happy.

Mr. Carlisle introduces three men who have joined him on the stage, and for forty minutes we listen to speeches. A doctor tells what AIDS is and how it's transmitted. His speech is pretty much what Dr. Patterson told me on Thursday, and again I feel reassured. The second man, from the

Board of Education, describes precautions schools have taken in other epidemics, and the third man, a lawyer, talks about the rights of students—the right to an education, the right to privacy. He stresses that none of us should even know Connie has AIDS. I begin to smile. The last two speeches make it pretty obvious that Connie will be staying in school. The audience, I notice, picks up on that, too. No one else, however, smiles. As soon as the third man sits down and Mr. Carlisle returns to the podium, questions begin.

The first comes from an angry man in the front row. "My daughter has gym class with this Connie Tibbs. They'll be playing contact sports, taking showers. I want to know exactly how my daughter will be protected."

"I think we've answered that." Mr. Carlisle nods toward the man from the Board of Education. "Mr. Simpson explained that the Board—"

"That's not enough." A woman halfway back in the audience stands up. "We're not talking about a new strain of flu. We're talking about AIDS."

"Yeah." People in various parts of the room support the woman's view.

"That's right."

"You tell 'em, sister!"

"And Mr. Carlisle, where does your child go to school?" another woman asks. "Not any place where there's AIDS, I bet."

"Please." Mr. Carlisle tries to regain control "Please!"

"I'm outta here," I say to Mike.

"Me too."

Outside the gym I pause, squinting as my eyes adjust to the autumn sunshine.

Mike is beside me on the steps. "Real bummer in there, isn't it?" For once he's talking like a regular person.

"Yeah," I agree. I look around and wonder. What I see is still a great day. Some marshmallow clouds have drifted across the blue sky. A breeze moves through the tops of trees and rattles the leaves. A half block away two little boys play on skateboards in a driveway. I stand there, looking at everything and wondering how there can be this absolutely terrific day outside and all that ugliness inside. "You know what really bothers me?" I say to Mike.

"What?"

"No one thinks about Connie as Connie anymore. All they think about is this person who has AIDS, and it just happens to be Connie."

"Mobs don't think about people," he says. "It's always been that way. Did you know—"

I hear the start of a history lesson and tune him out. I don't want any part of it. What I want is to yell and scream about those people back in the gym. I know they're scared. I know it's hard to believe the doctors—or any school official. But why do they

34 •

have to take their fear and frustration out on Connie? That's not fair.

"Mike," I begin, but he's still talking.

"My dad went to a lot of those marches for peace and stuff in the sixties. He says that even back then when people were super-concerned, they'd—"

"Oh, Mike!" There's this volcano in my throat. I know that in a moment it's going to explode and I'll wind up yelling. Doesn't Mike realize? The sixties were the sixties; this is now, and Connie Tibbs has AIDS. All the stories in the world, all the quotes Mike Rowen has ever read aren't going to make me feel one bit better about what's happening now. I open my mouth, ready to explain all that. And what comes out?

"Stop it, Mike," I hear myself saying in a voice that's way too loud. "Blow it out your ear. Take your nineteen-sixties and how this is like everything else and blow it all out your ear!" I dart down the steps and away.

chapter four

On Monday, as much from habit as anything else, I eat lunch with Rae. She's already in the cafeteria when I get there, so I sit down across the table from her and unload my tray. A tuna-fish sandwich. Potato chips. A slice of chocolate pie.

Rae looks at my pie and winces. "Just once, I wish you'd have to diet."

"Sorry." Actually I'm glad I don't. Rae's got this five pounds she's always gaining and losing. And gaining back again. It's a hassle.

I toss my tray on a rack near our table and dig into the pie. I've always thought meals taste better if you start with dessert. At home my mother objects. At school I indulge myself.

"So what'd you and Todd do this weekend?" Rae asks.

"Nothing much. Went to the movies. Yesterday I had dinner at his house."

Rae eats some lasagna. "I can't wait for next weekend."

"Yeah?" It takes a minute to remember. "Oh, yeah. The Back-to-School Dance." Todd and I have already made plans to attend with Rae and her sometimes steady boyfriend, Nick Jacoby.

"That's right, eraser brain, the Back-to-School Dance. Which is always held the second weekend after school starts. How could you forget?"

I shrug. "I didn't exactly forget. It just wasn't on my mind."

"It sure would be on mine," Rae says, "particularly if I had as good a chance of making the court as you do. Think you will?"

"I don't know." Every year the homecoming court is announced at the Back-to-School Dance, and I'd love to be on it. But I'm not holding my breath. "I'm only a junior."

"Juniors make the court. Sometimes. Besides, Nick says Todd talked you up real big with the tennis team."

"Yeah, but that was last spring. Probably then I would have made it. Now it'll be girls the football team wants. What about Nick? Isn't he pushing for you?"

"Sure. But it won't do any good. Not with Debbie McAllister badmouthing me all over the place."

I nod sympathetically. Debbie McAllister, our quarterback's current girlfriend, makes a lot of people's lives miserable. And it's been Rae's turn ever since Rae won a spot on the cheering squad and Debbie didn't.

"Oh, my gosh!" Rae says. "Look who's still here." She nods at something behind me.

I turn and see that Connie has just come off the serving line. She stands there, scanning the room, probably searching for a place to sit. But the cafeteria's crowded, and absolutely no one waves for her to join them. I wonder what she'll do.

"Guess Saturday's meeting didn't pan out," Rae says.

I ignore her and continue watching Connie.

She starts toward a table that has only three girls sitting at it. Immediately the girls bend down over their plates and start shoveling food into their mouths. By the time Connie reaches the table, they're finished. They leave, grabbing up their trays and striding past her without a word. She sits down, straightens her shoulders, and begins to eat.

At the table next to her are the kids I've been thinking of as her crowd. The guys wear their leather jackets; the girls have long hair and lots of makeup. I catch glimpses of painted fingernails, long enough in some cases to curl. Five minutes ago that table was noisy, its conversation punctuated with laughter and the occasional curse. Now, though, they all eat quietly and quickly. In a few minutes everyone leaves, and although they have to walk right past where Connie is sitting, no one speaks to her.

"She must be awfully lonely," I say.

"Don't waste your pity," Rae says. "She's bringing it on herself."

Rae's words startle me. "What exactly is she bringing on herself? You think she went out looking for AIDS?"

"No, but she doesn't have to come here and make herself miserable."

"What's she supposed to do?"

"Drop out. Stay home."

"Is she old enough to drop out? Don't you have to be seventeen? Or eighteen?"

"Come off it, Karen." Rae makes a noise that's close to a laugh. "What difference does her age make? She'll never need school."

In a flash I see what Rae's driving at and don't like it. "Maybe she wants to come."

"I sure wouldn't. Not if people were holding meetings to get rid of me."

"You're not her."

Connie gets up. On her way out of the cafeteria, she glances in my direction. I can tell she wants to smile, maybe even stop and speak. But I don't want her to. Not with everyone in the cafeteria watching. I look down at my plate and feel horribly guilty.

Rae hasn't noticed. She finishes off her container of milk and folds her straw down in it. "Thank heavens I'm not her. All I know is that we'd be a lot safer if she wasn't here."

"Really?" And now I'm angry. I don't know if I'm angry at Rae for what she's saying or at myself for not speaking to Connie, but I'm angry. "Last Wednesday you weren't sure about that. You said you didn't know if they should kick her out or not."

"Well, I've changed my mind. I've thought things over and talked to a lot of people."

"Obviously the wrong ones," I mutter.

Rae hears me. "Look, Karen, you might be dumb enough to keep her as your lab partner, but the rest of us have more sense."

"If having sense means being nasty to someone who's sick, I don't want any." I've had enough. It's obvious Rae isn't going to listen to reason any more than those people at Saturday's meeting would. I drop my napkin on the table, get up, and walk away. As I leave the cafeteria, I think about my half-eaten lunch, and I'm glad I ate the pie first.

The week passes. After Monday, Connie doesn't show up. And that has consequences. Gradually people start talking to me again, and by Friday things are pretty much back to normal. Saturday I'm more than ready for Todd, the Back-to-School Dance, and having a good time.

He picks me up a little after eight. He's wearing jeans and this really great sweater, a warm brown, that comes close to matching his eyes. He smells of after-shave lotion.

My mother looks from his jeans to mine, smiles, and shakes her head. "I don't understand this generation. Don't you kids ever dress up for anything?"

"Oh, Mom," I say.

"Oh, Karen," she mimics.

I shoot her a withering glance. Oh-Mom-Oh-Karen has become this game we play when we disagree about things. Minor things. What I ate for lunch. Did I watch too much TV? Or, like now, what I'm wearing.

"I am dressed up," I say. "I spent an hour putting this outfit together." In addition to the jeans, I've got on a plaid shirt, a big sweater that hangs down below my hips, two gold chains, and hoop earrings.

"I'm not sure the amount of time it takes to get ready translates into being dressed up." Mom's amused, trying hard to keep from laughing. "Actually I was looking for something totally different. A formal perhaps. Long white gloves?"

"I'll get a formal someday," I promise. I don't think you can wear blue jeans to the junior prom, but I haven't really checked into it. I take hold of Todd's arm. "Come on. Let's get out of here before she makes us look at pictures of how she used to dress." I smile so my mother will know I'm kidding. Truth is, most of the pictures she has of back when she and my dad were teenagers are pretty neat. But right now I want to go to the dance. We exchange good-byes, then Todd and I leave to pick up Rae and Nick.

When the four of us get to school, the dance is already under way. We pause just inside the dimly lit gymnasium. There's a refreshment table at one end of the room, a guy spinning discs at the other. Arranged in corners are pumpkins and bales of hay. Colored leaves decorate the bleachers, which have been pushed back against the wall. I smile, feeling secure and comfortable. I like traditions, and the Back-to-School Dance is as traditional as things get. Each year it has autumn leaves, Halloween pumpkins, and the promise of Thanksgiving and Christmas soon to come.

For about an hour Todd and I dance, drink punch that's too sweet, and eat cookies. After one number—an old Buddy Holly song from the fifties—the PA crackles on. Tony Phelps, president of the Student Government Association, climbs up on the DJ's stand and waves a piece of paper.

"It's here," he says, "the moment you've been waiting for." He pauses. "And what have you been waiting for?"

"The homecoming court," the crowd responds.

"I can't hear you," Tony teases.

"The homecoming court," we say again, this time really loud.

Tony grins and begins reading names. Squeals follow each one, and the girls join him onstage.

"You could be next," Todd says right after Tony announces Sara Strong.

I hang on to Todd's hand and try to tell myself that it doesn't matter, that five years from now no one will even remember who was on the court. But it doesn't work. I want my name to be called, and when it is, at first I don't believe it. I turn to Todd. "Did he . . . ?"

"Go for it, kid." Todd gives me a push in the direction of the stage.

And then I'm up there, hopping up and down with Sara and Joyce and Elise and Dorothy. We're it, and we know it. We're the prettiest, the most popular girls in school.

"Let's celebrate," Todd says, once the announcements are over and I've gone back down on the dance floor.

"Yeah!" And suddenly the dance seems like the place where fun only begins. "Let's have pizza and Cokes and then drive up to the lake."

"You're on." Todd slings an arm around my shoulders. We find Rae and Nick, and leave. Together, right then, all four of us are very happy.

Pizza Delight is crowded. Some of the kids I recognize as just having been at the dance. Others are older—probably from one of the local colleges. There are even two tables of adults.

Todd, Rae, Nick, and I lay claim to a corner booth designed to seat eight. At first our waiter complains, but we say three more people are coming. He shrugs and takes our order. I sense he doesn't believe us, but what can he do? Come right out and call us liars?

The evening stays fun. Everyone toasts me with Cokes and kids me about being the next homecoming queen. I kid back, saying that if I win, I won't be only a figurehead. I'll do a school first—I'll be a real queen. I'll claim power and pass all sorts of reforms. We joke about the changes we want. Rae pushes for being allowed to talk in the library. Not real loud talking, she explains, just whispering that wouldn't bother anyone. Todd thinks every teacher over forty should be fired, and Nick says football players should be excused from tests and home-work during football season.

"All that will happen," I promise, "but first I'm getting rid of lab courses." Thoughts of that frog I'll have to cut up continue to haunt me.

"Why?" Todd asks. "You shouldn't have any trouble with Bio now that your problem's gone."

"My problem?" I don't remember talking to him about the frog. And the frog certainly isn't gone.

"Yeah." Todd scrapes the mushrooms off a piece of pizza. "Now that Connie's dropped out of school."

"She hasn't dropped out," Rae says. "She's sick." She turns to Nick. "Didn't you tell me she'll be back sometime next week?"

Nick nods. "That's what I heard."

"Know what I think?" Todd's face contorts. "I think they should just go ahead and kick her out."

"Come on, Todd," I say, "you don't mean that."

"Yes, I do. She doesn't need to be in school. She's just gonna die."

"Todd!" I snap, hating how nasty he sounds and looks right then. "That's a horrible thing to say."

And we all know it is—even Todd. I can see in his eyes that he knows it, but he won't take it back. Or apologize. So we fall silent and sit there looking at the leftover pieces of pizza.

After a while I crumple my napkin and fling it down on the table. The fun has gone out of the evening, and I realize that the last few days have been a lull. Connie'll come back to school, I'll keep her as my lab partner, and things'll get messy all over again.

chapter five

Connie comes back to school on Wednesday. I hear she's there long before I see her, and I wonder if she's different, if being sick for a week has changed her. I remember pictures of Rock Hudson and a couple of TV movies about Liberace. Could she look that bad? No. Those guys were about to die, and Connie's . . . Connie's fine, I tell myself.

I get to Biology a few minutes early, and she's already there, sitting at our table. She doesn't see me watching her. Her Bio text is open. She reads, twisting a strand of blond hair around her index finger as she concentrates.

I walk over and sit down beside her. "Hi," I say. "How . . . ?" I stop myself. Should you ask someone with AIDS how she is? Now there's a point of etiquette Emily Post never covered.

Connie looks up, grinning. "It's okay. You can ask."

I relax. "How are you?"

"Okay now. I had a bug, but a bunch of drugs and six boring days in bed cleared it up."

I nod like I understand, but I really don't. The last time I had to stay in bed for that long was when I was ten and had some sort of flu. I colored and cut out paper dolls. I wonder how Connie filled the time. You can only watch so many soaps and reruns on TV; eight *Leave it to Beaver*'s are more than enough.

"You missed a lot," I say.

"I know." Connie riffles a few pages in her text and sighs. "I've been looking over the chapters you guys covered."

Guilt nibbles at me, and I scold myself for not having thought of taking her the homework assignments. Or if I didn't want to go over there, I could have at least called. Well, maybe I can do something now. "I've got an idea. Why don't we see if it's okay to work here after school? I can go over what we did."

"Would you?"

"Sure. If we can get Mr. Boggs to agree."

Mr. Boggs does, and Connie and I meet right after school. The classroom is quiet. Through closed windows we can hear the track and football teams practicing, but they're far away, and the sound is muted. Inside the room a wall clock hums. Occasionally a fly buzzes near our heads.

Connie and I go over two chapters in the text. I show her my lab notes, and we look at three slides Mr. Boggs left out for us.

"That wasn't too hard," she says once we've finished.

Is she surprised? She sure sounds like it. "Bio's not particularly hard," I say. "Sometimes it might be yucky," I add, thinking of the frog. "But not hard."

"Yeah, but you're not . . . "

I wait. She leaves the sentence alone, closes her book, and stuffs the slides back in their envelope.

"Not what?" I prompt.

She draws a faint breath. It's like she's started a conversation she doesn't really want to have but, at the same time, doesn't know how to stop. "You're not used to taking only business courses," she finally says.

"Oh, yeah." Working with Connie, seeing her in class, I've almost forgotten she was in a different program. I stack up my books. "Bio's not any worse than a lot of classes you guys take. Don't you have some math course that's really hard?"

"Accounting. But we never had to learn anything like that." She nods at a chart on the bulletin board that shows various species of plant and animal life. "Even the decorations in this class are scary."

I grin. "How come you're in Bio anyway? They haven't started requiring it for business students, have they?"

"No. I switched over to college prep."

"But why . . . ?" I stop.

"Why bother when I'll probably never go to college?" she guesses.

I nod. "You're pretty good at that."

"What?"

"Finishing things people start to say." I'm remembering my false start on "How are you?"

"Right now it's pretty easy. People—those who'll talk to me at all—don't know what to say. And for the most part it's obvious what they're thinking." Connie gets up, goes to the window, and stares out. From the courtyard below come discordant notes as the band begins tuning up for afternoon practice. "Besides, I've had this conversation about college prep before."

"Oh?"

"My mother asked the same thing you're asking. Why bother?"

"So what'd you tell her?"

Connie turns back around to face me. "That I was doing it because of her. All my life she compared me to Andy and LouAnn. With Andy it was brains. 'Your older brother's so much smarter than you are.' Never mind how much trouble he got into. And with LouAnn? Well, she was real popular. 'LouAnn's friends are so nice.' Meaning, of course, that mine weren't. Well, I'm probably not gonna get any new friends, but I am gonna find out if Andy really is smarter."

"So you're taking harder courses."

"Yeah." Her expression turns sheepish. "Maybe it is kind of dumb."

"I don't think so." Actually, I'm impressed. If I had AIDS, if I knew I wasn't going to live all that long, I don't know what I'd do. I'm pretty sure, though, that my game plan wouldn't include more studying. "The school give you any trouble about changing tracks?"

"At first." She shrugs. "Then I guess they decided it didn't matter which program I was in."

"Why not?"

"Think about it. I don't really need to be prepared for college. I don't even need to be prepared for business." She begins to smile. "Know what?"

"What?"

"I bet since grades no longer matter, my teachers all give me A's."

"Is this an advantage to having AIDS?" I ask.

"Sure. Forget about buying that encyclopedia. Forget about taking notes during class. The really safe way to good grades is to get an incurable disease. Then you don't even have to study."

We both laugh, then stop. It's funny, but it's not.

"Hey, Connie," I blurt out. "Can I ask you something?"

She hesitates, and immediately I wish I could take the words back. But it's been cool. She's seemed so open, so ready to talk about being sick. And I admit I'm curious. Not that that makes me different from anyone else in school. We're all curious.

So now I watch as her head rises and her chin juts forward. Instantly I'm reminded of a very determined eleven-year-old who on an April day became part of my life.

"Depends on what it is you want to ask," she says.

She's acting real cautious, and I figure she knows what I'm about to say. But I can't start the conversation over. With a breath I begin. "How'd you—"

"No!" she snaps. "You can't ask that."

A flash of inspiration, and I change where I was coming from. "How'd you like to stop by Burgers and More for a Coke?" I smile, hoping I haven't totally loused up the easiness that existed between us a minute ago. "That's what I was gonna ask."

The hostility fades; she grins back. "I knew that."

We leave, our footsteps echoing in the empty stairwell as we head down to the main entrance.

"About what you really started to ask back there," Connie says. "I don't want people to have anything else to talk about."

"I wasn't gonna talk about it."

Connie looks skeptical, and I can't say I blame her. We were friends for a couple of weeks; then we weren't friends for five years. I guess expecting her to trust me right off would be awfully unrealistic. But part of me wishes it weren't that way.

We step outside the school, and a car honks. I look to the right. There, among the few cars left in the student parking lot, is Clara Car.

"That's Todd," I say.

"I know."

"Well"—I think about his most recent references to Connie and force heartiness—"let's go see what he wants. Maybe we can all have that Coke together." But Clara Car is already moving backward. Gravel sprays as Todd switches to forward and peels out of the parking lot.

"Wonder what made him do that?" Connie's flippant tone masks a hurt.

I shrug, not saying anything. We both know what my answer would be.

"You sure about having that Coke?" she asks.

"Sure I'm sure." But I'm not. I can see people leaving if Connie and I show up together in Burgers and More. We walk in, we're labeled friends, and from then on the kids I've always known, the kids I've hung around with treat me differently. I don't want that. I like Connie; I want to spend time with her, but at the same time I still want to be popular.

"I'll see you tomorrow." Connie has been watching me and reaches a decision on her own.

Before I can protest, she takes off, and I start walking home. Slowly. There are just too many things to think about.

I'm three blocks away from school the next morning when Rae catches up with me. She grabs my elbow and propels me into Burgers and More. "We have to talk," she announces.

"Rae, I can't. I have a test second period, and I have to get to school early to study."

"This won't take long." She pushes me into a booth.

A waitress, dark hair pulled back in a bun, approaches. "What'll it be?"

"Nothing, thanks," Rae says. "We're just here for a minute." She turns back to me, dismissing the waitress.

But the waitress doesn't dismiss. "If you're gonna sit in a booth, you gotta order. Them's the rules."

I glance at my watch. "Rae, I—"

"Those sweet rolls." Ignoring me, Rae nods at the counter where two glass-covered pedestal dishes are filled with Danish. "Are they fresh?"

"Of course they're fresh."

"Then I'll take one."

The waitress leaves, and Rae moans. "So much for the diet. I really did start dieting this morning."

"You don't have to eat it. The rule is just that we have to order. Now could—"

"You're telling me to leave food on my plate?" Rae rolls her eyes. "What about the children starving in . . . " She frowns. "Where are the children starving this year?"

I wasn't about to let her go off on a tangent, not with that test looming. "You wanted to talk about something?"

"Todd. Thanks." That to the waitress, who returns with the Danish. "Cherry. My favorite. If she'd brought prune, I would have stood a chance. I might have been able to leave it. But not cherry."

Rae pulls the Danish in half and starts to eat, first nibbling at the cherry center.

Shoot. If Rae sets the pace, this conversation will take forever. So I prod. "What about Todd?"

"He wanted me to talk to you to see if you were angry."

"Why should I be angry?"

"I don't know. He says he did something yesterday that might have ticked you off."

"Yesterday?" I can't remember anything about yesterday. All I can think about is that test. "Rae, I didn't talk to Todd yesterday. I don't think I even— Oh." I left the school building with Connie. Todd tore out of the parking lot in Clara Car.

"You are mad at him."

"Sort of." Todd's being a jerk about Connie, but it's nothing I want to get into. At least not right now. I slide toward the edge of the booth. "If that's—"

"What'd he do?" Rae licks her fingers and goes after the second half of the Danish.

I give a quick sigh. "Nothing that bad. Saw me with Connie and took off."

Rae stops eating. "You're not really starting to hang around with her, are you?"

"I helped her with some Bio stuff she missed last week. Now, if—"

"It's not good to see a lot of her, Karen. It's really not. We've got friends." Rae pauses. "Good friends," she adds meaningfully.

For a second I frown. Then I understand what Rae's getting at, and anger stirs. I bounce back toward the center of the booth. "Do we?"

"Yes."

"We have *good* friends?" I say, letting myself sound sarcastic.

"Yes!" Impatience enters Rae's voice.

"Then what's the problem?"

"The problem," she begins, "is that if you and Connie get close, our friends—"

"Our good friends," I interrupt.

"Yes!" Rae's dark eyes go steely. "Our good friends."

"Won't have anything else to do with me?" If Rae's going to make threats, I want them out in the open. Out where we can both see how ugly they are.

"Karen." Rae hesitates, fingering her Danish, trying to bring her own emotions under control. "No one's comfortable with Connie around. No one—"

"Excuse me!" I hop up and snatch my books from the table. "My test. Remember?" Angry, I storm out and leave Rae sitting there, a piece of that dumb Danish held halfway to her mouth. I head for school, walking with large steps, taking deep breaths. I'll get my temper under control. I'll get to school early. And maybe I'll still have a little time to study.

Todd's waiting for me when I come out of my last class. He apologizes, we make a date for the weekend, and everything's okay.

Then, three days into the next week, nothing's okay. I'm standing beside Connie in Bio, staring down at broken glass. A slide has slipped out of her hand.

"I'll get it," she says, and reaches down. "Ouch!" She stands up, holding her index finger. "I cut myself."

She doesn't need to tell me. I can see that her finger's bleeding. Not a lot, just a few drops. But deadly drops, I realize. And then I'm transfixed. I stare at that bleeding finger. Somewhere in that blood, so tiny I can hardly imagine them, are cells gone wrong, cells containing viruses that could kill everyone in this room.

"Hand me a Kleenex," she says.

I don't move.

"Come on, Karen. I'll bleed all over everything." She looks up and sees that I'm standing there, frozen. Her face hardens. "Karen! I'm not gonna force my finger in your mouth. I'm not gonna smear blood all over you. I just want a Kleenex." She turns away, and a sound escapes her. A sob? Yes. An angry sob.

"Connie." I reach for her. "I—"

"Keep away from me! I don't need you, Karen Thompson." By now she's attracting attention. Kids who work near us are looking over, checking out what's going on. She glares at them. "I don't need any of you." She bolts from the room.

"Miss Thompson?" Mr. Boggs calls me up to his desk. "What happened?" he asks.

"Connie cut herself on a piece of glass."

"And caused all that turmoil?"

"She was bleeding."

"Still, I . . . Oh." Mr. Boggs has just remembered Connie has AIDS. "Yes. It would cause turmoil. But it's over. You can go back to your seat now."

I start back.

"Wait" He stops me. "Don't clean anything up. Maintenance will do it tonight. With gloves and things."

"Okay."

"And Karen?"

"Yes."

"Would you like another partner?"

I shake my head.

"It could be risky," he warns.

I shrug. It was risky when Connie pulled me out of the river all those years ago, but that didn't stop her.

"You're sure," he presses.

"I'm sure." But I'm not. Even with memories of that April day spread across my mind, part of me would still like a new partner. I just won't let myself have one.

At eight-twenty that night the phone rings.

Connie starts talking as soon as I answer. "I'm sorry," she says. "It's just that you're going along, thinking everything's normal. Maybe you've even forgotten that you're sick. Then something happens. Something simple. You cut your finger, and it's the end of the world. People back away from you like you've got some horrible disease. Which, of course, you do. And you realize you're a freak and that's all you'll ever be. But I'm sorry. I shouldn't have yelled at you. Or at them." She hangs up.

I try to finish reading a chapter in my History text, but I can't. Words and dates and who did what to whom just don't have a lot of meaning.

chapter six

My mother knocks on the bathroom door. "Todd's on the phone," she says.

"Tell him I'll be there in a sec." I've just finished washing my hair, and it's still wet. I wrap a towel around my head, slip on a robe, and hurry to pick up the extension in my bedroom.

"Doing anything tomorrow after school?" Todd asks.

"Not really."

"Could you take Joey to the dentist?"

"I guess so." It's an odd request. Joey is Todd's eight-year-old little brother. A perfectly ordinary, happy-go-lucky kid—except for the fact he's in a wheelchair. Todd, of course, is crazy about him, and really protective, usually ready to cart him anywhere he wants or needs to go. Even to the dentist. "Why aren't you taking him?"

"Screwed-up plans. Mom's out of town, Dad'll be at work, and Coach Leeds called a meeting of the tennis team."

"In October?"

"Yeah. It's something about how the team'll be selected this year."

I shrug. "Okay. Sure. I'll take him."

"You can use Clara. I'll get you in the morning and let you have the keys. Then after Joey's finished with the dentist, you can pick me up at school. Okay?"

"Okay."

We hang up, and I go back into the bathroom. It's not long before my mother knocks again.

"You about done in there?" she asks.

"Yeah." My hair's almost dry. I turn off the dryer, put it away, and stuff my towel in the hamper. "All yours," I say as I step out into the hallway.

"Actually, I didn't need the bathroom. I wanted to talk to you for a minute." She follows me into my room. "Is everything okay?"

"Sure." I look through my closet, trying to decide what to wear tomorrow. It's starting to turn cold now, and soon I'll have to make the big wardrobe switch. Winter stuff out of the attic, summer stuff in. "Why shouldn't everything be okay?"

"I don't know. I've been noticing some things lately, and Todd's call made me think of them."

"Like what?"

"Like the fact that the two of you aren't going out much." Mom's moving around the room, fixing things. She straightens a stack of papers on top of my bookcase, moves a porcelain ballet dancer an inch to the right on top of my bureau. I can tell she's not real comfortable with the conversation.

"Todd and I went out Saturday," I say. "Twice the weekend before."

"You never study together anymore."

"We're in different classes." I sit down at my dresser and begin brushing my hair.

"And Rae hasn't called in ages."

I shrug. There's no way I can argue that one.

"Karen," my mother says, her gray eyes serious, "I'd hate to see you stop being friends with those two. You've all been friends for so long, and it's always seemed so right."

"Right?" Is my-mother-the-snob rearing her ugly head again?

"The three of you have always gotten along so well," she amends.

Silent, I decide to accept my mother at her word.

She goes on. "I know that with expanding the shop, I'm not around much, but you can still talk to me if there's something wrong. You know that, don't you?"

"There's nothing wrong," I say. But there is. I put my brush back down on the dresser. Slowly, steadily, I'm becoming a social outcast because of a friendship with Connie Tibbs. Am I ready to tell my mother that? No way. We went down that road together a long time ago. I'm not real interested in traveling it again.

It feels funny having the keys to Clara Car in my pocket. They press against me whenever I sit down, and I pretend that they're keys to my own car. A car that, as Todd did, I got on my last birthday. It's a nice dream, and I'm deep into it when Roberta Phillips—this geek of the female persuasion—comes up to me in the library.

She sits down and whispers, "There's trouble over near the main entrance. You might be able to help."

"What sort of trouble?" I ask.

"Just come with me."

I pick up my books and follow her out of the library.

About twenty students have gathered in the hallway. They're watching something and talking among themselves. Roberta pushes her way through the crowd; I trail in her wake.

"Oh, no," I mutter when I see that Connie's on the floor, her books scattered around her.

"Please, someone," she's saying, "help me up. Just help me up, and I'll go."

No one moves.

How can they do it? How can they just stand there? Surely someone could have done something. At least gone for help, if not gotten involved. I elbow my way between two guys.

"Hey," one of them says, "it's Supergirl to the rescue."

I glance back and see Clyde Wilson leering at me. "Shut up!" I say. Is he always going to be nasty to Connie? Won't he ever let up?

"Better be careful," he warns, "or you'll get sick and everyone'll know you do the same things Connie does. Maybe you even do them together."

I ignore him and move on over to Connie. "Come on," I say. "Hang on to me."

"My legs got real weak. Then they stopped working. Karen, I'm so tired."

"It'll be okay." I loop one of her arms around my neck and pull her up. It's easy. She hardly weighs anything. Once she's on her feet, I glare at the crowd, hoping no one will see the tears that have formed in my eyes. "Couldn't one of you have helped her?" Silly question. Still, I go on and add, "It wouldn't have hurt you."

Supporting Connie, I push my way back through the crowd. People move away at the first step I take in their direction. It's like they think the slightest touch of Connie—or me—will contaminate them.

I can see the door to the nurse's office standing open at the end of the hallway. It looks like it's miles away, and I'm tired by the time we get there. Connie may be losing weight, but she's still a lot heavier than things I'm used to carrying around. Like a book bag. Or even my five-gallon floppy purse.

"Thanks," she mutters as I slip her into a seat in the waiting room.

"You'll pay me back," I say. "Three miles on a bicycle for two, with you doing all the work."

She manages a smile.

"Yes?" The nurse enters from a back room, and I'm comforted by her presence. Everything she has on is white. Her cap, her uniform, even her shoes and stockings. Surely anyone who looks that medical will know what to do.

She sits at her desk, her smile polite and professional. "May I help you?"

"My friend"—I nod at Connie—"got real weak and fell down."

"Fainted?"

"Not exactly. At least I don't think so."

She addresses Connie. "Did you eat breakfast this morning, dear?"

Connie mumbles a response.

"She said yes," I say.

"An adequate breakfast? Or just some sort of snack? So many of you girls try to lose weight by cutting back on breakfast, and that's not the way to diet. Not at all." There's a briskness about the woman that translates into competence. I like that.

I nudge Connie. "What'd you have for breakfast?"

Another mumble.

"Toast," I say.

The nurse starts to frown. "Not the best breakfast, but surely enough to keep someone from fainting. What about physical activity? Have you had gym this morning?"

Again Connie mumbles, this time a longer mumble, and I strain to listen. "She had gym at nine, but they watched a film." I'm beginning to feel like a ventriloquist with a rather uncooperative dummy. Still, the audience isn't bad. The nurse hasn't gotten up and left. Or thrown a tomato.

"Well, that lets out the two most obvious reasons for this weakness. I guess we'll just have to take a look. Let me fill out a form about when you came in and why, then I'll take your friend into the examining room." The nurse pulls a piece of paper out of a desk drawer. "Name?"

"My name or my friend's?" I ask.

"Your friend's."

"Connie Tibbs."

The nurse freezes, her pen held above the top line of the form. She doesn't look up. "I'm afraid I can't help you." Her voice is softer now but has an edge.

"Why can't you?" A knot forms in my stomach, and I'm scared. "She needs help. Look how weak she is." Connie has slumped over. Her eyes are closed; her chin almost touches her chest.

"You and I both know," the nurse says, "that her weakness is only a symptom."

"Okay. So she has AIDS. You're still a nurse."

"I'm a part-time nurse in a school. I have a family. Three kids. I can't take the risk."

"Doctors and nurses are supposed to take risks." I know that. Memories of books I read when I was little flash through my mind. Books about Clara Barton. Florence Nightingale. A series about a nurse. Sue somebody.

"I'm sorry." The school nurse—a far cry from my memories of Sue somebody—still concentrates on what's on her desk. She puts her pen down. She riffles through a stack of manila folders, glancing at the label on each one.

"Please!" I say.

The nurse, without even looking up, shakes her head. She makes a shooing gesture, as if to send Connie and me to the door. "Now if you'll—"

My temper snaps. "Leave? Oh, yes, we'll gladly leave!" The knot in my stomach is hard now. Nothing's the way it's supposed to be. "Come on, Connie. Let's go. It's stupid to hang around here any longer."

"Stupid?" the nurse asks, her voice sharp.

"Stupid!" I'm losing it, and I just don't care. "We come in here—"

"Really." The woman's back straightens. "I see no need to shout."

"And I see no need for a nurse who won't help people. The only reason you're here is to help kids who get sick and—"

"Hold on, young lady! I don't have to listen to this. I'm sure your guidance counselor—"

"Never mind! Forget it! We're out of here." Blood racing, I maneuver Connie up from her seat and out into the hallway. I prop her against a wall. Will she stay? I watch to see if she falls to one side or the other, like some sick imitation of the Tin Man in

The Wizard of Oz, but she remains stationary. Thank goodness for that.

Now what? I force myself to calm down. The argument with the nurse is in the past. It happened. There's nothing I can do about it now.

I look around; the horror of where I am and what I'm doing settles over me. It's a nightmare. I'm alone in a school hallway; a nurse is ready to report me to a guidance counselor; a limp Connie Tibbs leans against the wall beside me. Is the wall supporting Connie, or is she supporting it? If I move her, will the wall come tumbling down? I giggle, then stop. It's not funny. I realize I'm getting hysterical and try to come up with a plan.

What should I do? Get help, obviously. But where? And who? Someone connected with the school? No way. That could be the nurse all over again. Outside help? We have to qualify as an emergency. Of course! An ambulance! I could call an ambulance. Yeah. I'll get Connie to the pay phones—second floor, far end of the building. Then I'll call an ambulance. Then we'll come back down here and wait. Sure. Whole thing shouldn't take more than an hour. My initial elation fades. Maybe she'll still be conscious by then. I look at her. Semiconscious? That's a lot closer to what she is now.

"Come on, Connie. We're going on a journey." I pull her away from the wall and loop her arm around my shoulders. "We're on the *Enterprise*, searching for Klingons. We're hobbits, off to Mordor."

Six steps later Connie's hip grazes against mine. Ouch! The contact is a lot sharper than I would have expected, and I realize why. It isn't only Connie's hip that I bump up against: It's the keys to Clara Car. I stop, reach into my pocket, and pull them out. Forget the ambulance! Connie and I are on our way.

The people in the hospital's emergency room are a lot more cooperative than the school nurse, and soon Connie's settled in a room. She falls asleep immediately. Even though her mother has been called and will be here as soon as possible, I decide to stick around. If Connie wakes up, I don't want her to be alone.

For a while I look out the window. To my right is the river that runs through the center of town, the river where Connie . . . Quickly I close off that line of thought. To my left is another wing of the hospital. I notice a window decorated with pumpkins, ghosts, and a witch. I imagine a kid inside, then try not to think about that either. Even Connie is way too young to be in a hospital.

"Hey, Connie," I say, "how 'bout some TV?" Of course she doesn't answer. I turn it on anyway and flip through channels. "Looks like we've got soaps, a game show, a movie, or reruns. I vote soaps first, then reruns." I sit down beside her bed and begin to watch. There's most of *General Hospital*, an Andy Griffith I've seen three times before, and Patty Duke.

A Cosby rerun is halfway over when a woman comes into the room. Her hair is blonder than Connie's, and she's wearing a skirt that's a little too short, a sweater that's a little too tight.

I stand up. "Mrs. Tibbs?"

"Yes." She crosses to the bed and looks down at Connie.

"I'm Karen Thompson," I say. "A friend of Connie's from school. I brought her here."

"Has a doctor seen her?"

"Yes. He'll be back later. The nurse said Connie's okay now. I mean she's not in a coma or anything. She's just sleeping."

Mrs. Tibbs gives a slight nod but remains focused on Connie. I guess she heard me all right.

A silence lengthens, and I start to feel uncomfortable. "I'll go now," I say, edging toward the door. "You're here, and I have things to do."

Things to do? The words trigger memory, and I hurry out of the room and out of the hospital. Boy, do I have things to do. Or, more accurately, things I should have done. I picture Joey, waiting at home to go to the dentist. I picture Todd, waiting at school for me to pick him up. Neither is a pretty sight.

It's almost dark when I arrive at school. Todd's pacing back and forth at one end of the parking lot. I pull up beside him, stop, and slip over into the passenger's seat.

He opens the door on the driver's side. "Karen, do you have any idea what time it is? What took you so . . . ?" He's looking in the backseat. "Okay. Where's Joey? Did you take him home already?"

"Todd, I never got him."

"What?"

I explain about Connie getting sick.

"I know about that," Todd says. "But so what?"

"I took her to the hospital, and I couldn't leave her alone. I waited until her mother got there. Then I came right here."

"You're telling me Joey never went to the dentist?"

"Yes."

"And that you used Clara Car to take Connie to the hospital?"

"Yes."

"Geez, Karen!" Todd jumps into the car. Gears grind as he slams into reverse; tires spin as he backs up over gravel. "I lend you Clara so you can take Joey to the dentist. But what do you do? You—"

I stop listening. Sure, Todd's angry. But I'm angry, too. Couldn't he at least try to understand?

"Karen." We're out on the road now and he sounds calmer. It's a controlled calm, but it is calm. "I can't take this any longer," he says. "You're letting everyone down. We hardly ever see each other. Rae hasn't talked to you in ages. Even

Miss Barslow's been looking for you. I saw her over at the gym the other day, and she asked if I knew why you'd missed cheerleading practice three times."

"I've been busy."

"Yeah. Busy running around with a girl who's eventually gonna kill us all. Karen, I want out of it."

A knot forms in my stomach, and I wonder if I'm hearing him right. "Out of what?"

"Us."

"We're breaking up?" I'm surprised when my voice squeaks.

"Yes."

"Because I helped someone who's sick? Todd, you can't be that cruel."

"I'm not being cruel. I'm taking you home. Being cruel would be leaving you standing in the school parking lot for hours."

I don't answer. I'm too stunned to answer. I turn and stare out the window. We're driving through downtown. Rush hour's almost over. Most of the parking lots have emptied out; only a remaining few shoppers straggle in and out of stores. After a while I glance back over at Todd. He looks straight ahead and grips the steering wheel with a tension that runs up his arms. I exhale a long, steady breath, then shrug. I don't have anything else to say to him, and I guess he feels the same. We drive the rest of the way home in silence.

chapter seven

❧ The door to Connie's hospital room is closed.
I stand there in the hallway, holding a bag of gourmet jelly beans, a single rose in a skinny green vase,
and a stuffed alligator whose beanie cap says Get
Well. I know the message isn't quite right—Connie
won't get really well—but he's wearing a State Uni-
versity T-shirt and carrying a football banner. I
think maybe he'll help Connie keep her mind on
college and positive stuff.

A nurse comes out of Connie's room and closes
the door.

"Ma'am," I say, "is it okay to go in there?"

"Oh, yes," she says with a smile. "I've been hoping my patient would have some company." She
bustles off toward the nurses' station.

I go into the room. Connie's sitting on the edge of
the bed. Her feet dangle, not quite touching the
floor. She has on a blue terry-cloth robe that's probably two sizes too large for her. She looks little and
forlorn.

Rock 'n' roll music blares out from the TV, and I step around so I can see what she's watching. "MTV?" I ask.

"Oh." She starts slightly. "I didn't hear you come in. Yeah. It's MTV."

"I couldn't get it two days ago."

"It costs extra. My brother sprang for it as a get-well present." She frowns. "Two days ago?"

"I brought you here. Hung around until your mother showed up. She seemed kind of . . ." I hesitate, unsure what word would best describe Mrs. Tibbs's behavior. "Remote?" I try.

Connie shrugs. "She's isn't handling all this real well."

"The AIDS?" I ask.

"Yeah. She doesn't want . . . She . . ." There's a silence. Then Connie goes on. "You know, I don't remember a lot about two days ago."

"You were pretty out of it." I sit in the chair beside the bed. "You're gonna be okay, aren't you?"

"Yeah. I should get to go home tomorrow."

"That's great." And it is great. So why does my voice sound hollow? And why does everything feel so stilted? Do Connie and I get along only when we're hunkered down over a microscope? "I brought you some stuff," I say.

"Oh? You mean alligators and flowers aren't part of your outfit? Accessories the well-dressed teenager is supposed to carry?"

I grin, and things ease out a little. I present my gifts, starting with the rose. "This is for decoration." I put it on the windowsill. "And now the room looks like . . ." I glance around. Even with the rose, it's still clearly a room in an institution, any institution. Beige walls. An orange vinyl chair. The TV mounted in the corner.

Connie finishes the sentence for me. "It looks like a hospital room with a rose."

We move on to the other things. She likes the alligator, but looks puzzled when she peers into the bag of candy.

"Jelly beans," I tell her.

"They're so little."

"They're fancy ones. Gourmet. That means they can be little and cost a lot."

"Is that why people buy them? I don't get it."

"The deal is they come in weird flavors. Gooseberry. Pumpkin. Peanut butter. Or you can combine them. Eat a chocolate and a peanut butter together, and you've got a peanut butter cup."

"Wouldn't it be easier just to buy one of those?"

"I did that, too." I pull a peanut butter cup out of my pocket and put it on her table. "I figured you could run a taste test."

"Forget tests. Peanut butter cups are my absolute favorite candy." She unwraps it, lifts it halfway to her mouth, then stops. She puts it back down on her table. "Let's go for a walk."

"Aren't you gonna eat that?"

"Maybe later. I'm not real hungry now."

I shrug. No wonder she's losing weight.

Connie finds her slippers, and we head out into a hallway that's actually kind of crowded. Two men, one in a white coat, the other in a business suit, study a patient's chart. A nurse carries medicine into a room. An elderly man, accompanied by a woman wearing blue jeans and a sweatshirt, walks slowly, holding on to his IV. Connie avoids looking at him, and I imagine she's thinking there'll be a time when she has to have stuff dripped into her. The thought makes me uncomfortable. I guess I'm just not used to visiting people in the hospital. And I can't say I like it a whole lot.

"So what happened two days ago?" I ask.

"I was doing too much."

"So they made you rest?"

Connie nods. "And they did some tests."

"For what?"

"My white count." I guess I'm frowning or something, because she goes on and explains. "That's part of the blood."

"And is it okay?"

"It's okay. Not great, but okay."

We loop twice around the floor, talking about Connie's white count, how the various nurses treat her, and what's happening at school. We go back into her room. It looks the same. Beige. Institutional furniture. A rose on the windowsill that doesn't improve the place one bit.

"So you get to go home tomorrow, huh?" I ask.

I guess she's picked up on my opinion of the room. "What's the matter?" she says. "Don't you like my surroundings?"

"They're okay. Not great, but okay."

She climbs back onto the bed, moving slowly. I can tell the walk wore her out. I hover near the door, figuring it's time for me to leave.

"Do me a favor?" she asks once she's settled.

"What?"

"Find out my homework assignments and bring them to me. Even if I get out of here tomorrow, it'll still be a few days before I can go back to school."

"Sure." I make a list of her classes and teachers. I have my hand out, ready to pull the door open, when she speaks again.

"There was only this one guy, you know."

"What?" I have no idea what she's talking about.

"A while back you wanted to ask how I got AIDS, and I wouldn't let you. Well, now I'm telling you."

I move back to the bed.

"I want you to know I didn't get it because of anything I set out deliberately to do. I wasn't doing drugs. And I wasn't sleeping around. I don't do that." The last is said sort of belligerently.

I'm surprised at her vehemence. "But at school," I blurt out. "The kids—"

"The kids," Connie interrupts, "believe what they want. You live on Twelfth Avenue, you take drugs. If your hair's long and blond and you don't pull it back in a dumb ponytail, you sleep around. You know that's junk, don't you?"

I nod.

Connie takes a breath. "Anyway, a couple years back . . ." She stops and starts again. "There was a guy . . ."

I can see that she's getting upset. "Connie, you don't have to—"

"I want to. I don't care what most of the kids at school think of me, but you're different." Her legs are sticking straight out on the bed. For a time she just sits there, breathing very regularly, watching her toes. Then she goes on. "There was this guy. He went to another school, but we met and started dating. I liked him. Really, really liked him. So after a while, we . . . You know." Connie stares down. Her hands are in her lap, her fingers extended. "And in some ways it was really great, being that close to someone. But we had to sneak around and look for places and stuff. I started feeling cheap and wanted to stop. But you can't just stop that sort of thing, so we wound up breaking up."

"And that's how you got AIDS?"

"I saw in the newspaper that he died and wondered how. Then last summer when I was sick and got tested . . ." Connie shrugs, then looks up at me.

"But I loved him, Karen. I really did. And I trusted him."

Geez. I'm thinking that if it was like that, anyone can wind up with AIDS. Most of the girls I know have fallen in love, at least once. And some of them have even done it. But AIDS? We never think about AIDS. "So how'd he get it?" I ask.

"I don't know. He was older. Maybe he'd played around with drugs. He was on the football team. My brother told me that sometimes athletes shoot up with steroids."

"So this guy . . . Maybe just once . . ." It's all too weird. "And now he's . . ."

"Dead," Connie fills in.

I hear her say the word, and there's a nasty, open spot at the pit of my stomach. AIDS kills people. And not just people generally. Real, specific people. People other people know.

"Hey!" Connie says. She sounds sort of alarmed, and I guess my expression has gone spacy. "I didn't tell you all this because I wanted you to do anything. Or to feel sorry for me. I just told you 'cause . . ." She's slowing down now. "Well, you know." She ends with a shrug.

I do know. Connie and I are becoming friends again, and you want your friends—your real ones at least—to know the truth about you. But you can't put things like that into words. It's too corny. "Yeah," I say, moving toward the door, "I know.

Look. I'll check those assignments and see you tomorrow. Here or home?"

"Call."

I leave. A rack filled with dinner trays stands in the hallway. I hold my breath, sickened by the combined smells of food and medicine, and run for the elevator. Once outside, I take great gulps of air and try not to think about what Connie told me. It's just too scary.

The next day I don't have to go back to the hospital. Connie's home, and, yes, it's the same address that bothered my mother all those years ago. I'm just glad it doesn't bother me.

So in the afternoon, right after school, I catch a bus to Mill Village. That's what people call Connie's part of town. And in a lot of ways my mother's right: It is kind of scuzzy. It's a ten-block area filled with wooden duplexes. The people who live there used to work at this mill that's right in the center of all the houses. Then the mill closed. Now, I guess, the people just live there and work somewhere else.

Connie's house looks like all the others. It has a tiny lawn—bigger than a postage stamp but not much—that could use a good seeding. The sidewalk in front of it is cracked and littered with toys that I imagine belong to the people next door. I skirt a yellow Big Wheel, mount three rickety steps to the porch, knock, and wait. Inside someone's talking, and I knock again. Footsteps replace the voice, and the inner door opens.

Mrs. Tibbs, this time dressed in tight blue jeans and a really scoop-necked T-shirt, squints out at me through the storm door. "Yes?" There's no sign that she recognizes me.

"I'm Karen Thompson," I explain. "Connie asked me to bring her some schoolwork."

"Oh, yeah. I forgot you were coming." Mrs. Tibbs opens the door and gestures that I should come in.

I do, stepping into a hallway that smells of stale cigarette smoke and a million different dinners.

"Connie's upstairs in her room," Mrs. Tibbs says. "You can go on up."

"Thanks." I start upstairs.

Mrs. Tibbs goes into the living room and resumes a conversation. "I can't keep staying home with her like this," she says. "Another three days, and that'll be my job."

I make a mental comparison and cringe. Sure, my mother and I have problems, but if I were sick— really, really sick—I know she'd be a lot more worried about me than some job.

Mrs. Tibbs is still talking. "I can't lose that job. There's the insurance. All the medical bills. I've—"

I hurry upstairs, hoping Connie can't hear the conversation. Once on the second floor, I decide it's a pretty safe bet she can't. A stereo blares, and I have to knock four times before she opens her door.

"Sorry," she says. "I've been playing this ever since I got home. That hospital was so quiet." She turns down the volume.

"I brought your assignments."

"Thanks."

I smile at her, she smiles at me, and we're off to another rip-roaring conversation. "Want me to go over what the teachers said?" I offer.

"If you've got time."

"I've got time."

She settles down at her desk. I sit on the edge of the bed, a couple of inches away. We cover Biology and move on to English. While Connie looks over some questions she'll have to answer about a short story, I hear her mother moving around downstairs. A few minutes later the phone rings.

"Connie?" Mrs. Tibbs calls. "It's for you."

"Back in a sec." Connie leaves; I hear footsteps as she tromps downstairs.

I wait. Time lengthens, and I begin to poke around the room. Not to pry, just to amuse myself. Or maybe that's still prying. I decide not to think about it.

On the wall are pictures of Tom Cruise, Emilio Estevez, and the rest of Hollywood's Brat Pack. There's a poster from the movie *St. Elmo's Fire*. The bookcase holds a few teenage romances, a lot of magazines, and a stack of college catalogues. I thumb through them and smile. Yale. Harvard.

M.I.T. Connie's dreaming, and she's dreaming big.

Footsteps pound up the stairs, and she bursts back into the room. "Guess who that was."

"Matt Dillon? Rob Lowe?"

"Rick!" She takes a pillow from the bed and dances around the room with it.

"Rick?"

"Rick Gillespie." She stops dancing. "That's right. You don't know about Rick. You know, it's strange. After these past few weeks, I keep thinking we know everything about each other. But we really don't, do we?"

"No."

"Rick's this guy I hung out with three summers ago. Here." She swoops over to the dresser, pulls a picture out from the edge of the mirror, and brings it to me.

It's a school picture of a guy with dark hair and blue eyes. He isn't smiling, but then a lot of kids refuse to smile for their school pictures. I'm not exactly the circus's laughing lady in mine. "Nice," I say, returning the picture to Connie.

She takes it back to the dresser. "We were super friends. We did everything. Went to the beach. Saw movies. Rented tapes. He stole that poster for me." She nods at *St. Elmo's Fire*. Then her expression changes. "I guess that doesn't sound real great, but it was a blast when he did it."

"And he's the one who called?"

"Yeah. Right after that summer his dad got laid

off from his job, and they moved. He's back in town for a few days, and I'm the first person he called. He's gonna see a couple of the guys, then come over here. And you know what's really great?"

"What?"

"He didn't even mention AIDS. We had this nice conversation that was perfectly normal. Just like I wasn't even sick."

"You're the first person he called?" I say without thinking, then wish I hadn't.

Connie's face clouds. Her lips tighten. She flops down on the bed and pulls the pillow over her stomach. "He doesn't know. He's gonna hear about it from the guys, and that'll be it."

"No!" I talk fast. This is the first time I've seen Connie really happy, and I don't want that happiness to vanish. "He probably knows. Where's he staying?"

"With an aunt."

"You know her?"

"I met her a couple times."

"And she knew the two of you were dating?"

Connie nods.

"Then she would have told him you have AIDS. You're not exactly a well-kept secret. Come on." I grab Connie's hand and pull her off the bed. "Let's wash your hair. We'll have you looking really great by the time he gets here."

And we do. We wash Connie's hair and trim a lit-

tle off the bangs. We experiment with makeup.
Then, to fill the time, we bake cookies. And play
Monopoly. And War. When I leave at seven—
already half an hour late for dinner—Rick still
hasn't shown up. We both know he's not going to,
but we don't talk about it. In fact, after I blurt out
that dumb thing about Connie being the first person he called, we never mention his name again.
Not even once.

chapter eight

On a weeknight the downtown library looks a lot like the one at school. Adults have abandoned ship, leaving the place to kids who usually study, sometimes giggle, and occasionally—I hate to admit it—throw spitballs.

Right now, on a Tuesday, I'm sitting at a table in the reference section, working on a history paper, and Mike Rowen comes up to me. I haven't seen him since that nasty meeting back in September, and I'm not real sure I want to now.

"Hey, Karen," he whispers, running his hand through his almost-red hair, "there's a guy in my Forms of Government class who wants to meet you."

"Okay." I'm surprised, and a little suspicious. Since I've been hanging around with Connie, most kids aren't even speaking to me. When someone does, it's usually to say something nasty. No one, but *no one*, has expressed any interest in meeting me.

"He's outside," Mike says.

I frown. "You mean I'm supposed to drop what I'm doing and go talk to him now?"

"He was hoping you would."

"Forget it. Let him talk to me at school."

Mike slips into the seat beside me. "He doesn't want to do that."

"Why? He's afraid someone'll see him talking to me and decide he's poison, too?"

"I don't think so. I think he's just shy." Mike's gaze is steady, really focused on me. "Please, Karen," he urges.

I realize he isn't going to go away. "Oh, all right. But this better be quick. The paper I'm working on is due tomorrow."

Mike follows me out of the reference area, through the library's domed center where the card catalogue and checkout desks are located. "Who is this guy?" I ask once it's safe to talk at a regular volume.

"Charles Bronson."

"Charles Bronson?"

"Not THE Charles Bronson. Another Charles Bronson. Charles?"

We're outside on a patio where in nice weather people eat sandwiches at small tables or sit on stone benches and talk. Now, though, in mid-November, the patio is almost deserted. Two children scuff through piles of leaves. A woman, huddled down in her coat, watches them and smokes a cigarette.

"Charles?" Mike calls again.

A guy emerges from the shadows and stands in the light that spills out through the library's glass doors. I squelch a smile. Mike's right. This is another Charles Bronson. He's tall and skinny. He has dark hair that's either tousled or curly—I can't tell which. And I have no idea what color his eyes are. All I can see is that they're behind dark-framed glasses that he keeps pushing up on the bridge of his nose with the index finger of his right hand. Dangling from his left hand is a briefcase that bumps against his knee with every step he takes.

"Karen," Mike says, "this is Charles Bronson. Charles, Karen Thompson. I'll leave you guys alone." And Mike is gone.

"Hi," I say, trying not to laugh.

"All right." Charles's lean face has a long-suffering look, like he's about to go through something he's been through a hundred times before. "Let's cut to the chase."

"What chase?"

"About my name. I know it's weird. I know I look wrong. Now you go ahead and laugh. Then I'll smooth things over. I'll tell you that Charles Bronson wasn't that big when I was born, that my father—my real father, that is—probably never saw one of his films. He was into things with subtitles."

"Your *real* father?" I ask.

"As opposed to my stepfather. Or any number of 'uncles' who've come to stay since my parents were divorced."

I feel a flash of sympathy. This guy has problems. At least after my father left, my mother never tried to replace him. "Mike said you wanted to meet me."

"Yeah." Charles switches his briefcase from his left hand to his right. "Is it okay if we sit down?"

I shrug and move to one of the stone benches. Charles follows and sits beside me.

"I wanted to talk to you about Connie Tibbs," he says.

What else? I slump down and fold my arms.

"You are friends with her, aren't you?" he asks.

"Yes. And she's not doing anyone any harm. She's not contagious. At least not in any ordinary sense."

"I know that."

Charles sounds very matter-of-fact, and it surprises me. "Then why do you want to talk about her?"

"I like her."

"Like her?"

"Yeah." Charles takes off his glasses, wipes each lens carefully with his handkerchief, and puts them back on. "I've liked her ever since we were in the eighth grade."

Eighth grade? That means I've been going to the same schools as Charles Bronson for more than three years and never even seen him? Talk about blending into the woodwork! This guy has it down to a science. "Did something special happen in the eighth grade?" I ask.

"She helped me out of a jam."

I wait.

"I was new then," Charles explains. "A bunch of kids were picking on me because of my name and how I looked. She got them to stop."

I can see Connie doing that. "And now?"

Charles pulls his glasses a couple of inches away from his nose, peers through them, then takes them off and wipes them again. "Now I'd like to ask her out."

"Out?" It dawns on me I'm doing a lot of echoing in this conversation and rephrase my response. "You mean like on a date?"

"Yeah. That is, if she's not going with anyone."

"She's not." That's the understatement of the year.

"I didn't think so. Most of her friends just kind of walked away, didn't they?"

"Forget 'kind of.' That's exactly what they did." I'm warming to the idea of Charles asking Connie out. What with Rick not showing up a few weeks ago and a couple of other slights from so-called friends, being asked out might be just what Connie needs. "So what do you want me to do?"

"Well." Behind his glasses, Charles blinks. He reaches up to take them off.

"Stop it!" I screech.

"What?"

"Your glasses. They're clean. They have to be clean."

"Oh." Charles leaves his glasses alone and stuffs the handerchief in a pocket. He sighs. "You see, that's the problem."

"What is?"

"I'm nervous just talking about this. And you're not even Connie."

"So?"

"So I thought maybe you could pave the way. See if she'd be willing to go out with me at all."

I look away. The lady has finished her cigarette and is herding the two little girls back into the library. Usually I don't like to get involved in other people's romantic problems, but this is different. After all, I wouldn't be matchmaking—I sure didn't go out looking for Charles. And Connie does need a boost. "Okay. I'll do it."

Charles is again reaching for his glasses. "I really hate to ask, but—"

"Charles!" I interrupt. "I said I'd do it."

"You did?"

"Yes!"

Charles's smile of relief tells me how difficult it was for him to ask. I think about him blending into the woodwork for so many years, and I think about all the kids who do just that. Kids who aren't on teams, who aren't elected to student government, who aren't working on the newspaper. Kids who, in a word, aren't. Being a cheerleader and running with kids who do things sure puts you in your own special world.

"Gee," Charles is saying, "this is great. I never really thought you'd agree, and—"

"Okay, okay." I stand up, more than ready to get away. His gratitude is embarrassing. "I'll talk to Connie tomorrow, but right now I have to get to work."

Charles nods.

I smile and hurry back into the library.

Connie and I have gone to her house to study. She's in the kitchen, fixing some sort of snack. I'm upstairs in her room, camped out on the floor, waiting. I paw through her record collection. Billy Joel. Bruce Springsteen. George Michaels. Not as far out as I expected. I sit back on my heels. As soon as she comes up, I'll have to talk to her about Charles.

She pushes open the door and enters, balancing a tray filled with sandwiches, apples, two slices of pie, and milk. "One good thing about AIDS," she says, "is you don't have to watch your weight."

I grin. We've been playing one-good-thing-about-AIDS ever since we kidded around about illness being a way to get good grades without studying. "Yeah," I say, "you can eat all you want, and you don't even have to drink eight glasses of water a day. Remember when everyone was on that diet?"

Connie nods. "You couldn't get into the bathroom."

"I knew three girls who snuck into the boys' room once 'cause it was closer."

"For real?"

"For real," I say, and we both laugh.

Connie sits at the desk and picks up a sandwich. She eats two bites, then puts it back down. "Of course you lose weight 'cause nothing tastes right. And that's no fun at all." She shrugs. "Come on. Let's study." She pushes the plate to one side and reaches for her Bio book.

"Wait." An image of Charles Bronson looms before me, and I know it's time. I have to do it. "Connie, we need to talk about something first." I get up off the floor and perch on the edge of the bed. "Do you ever think about going out?"

For a moment she just stares at me. Then: "I go out all the time," she hedges. "There's school. And I have appointments with doctors. You know how many doctors I see."

"I meant with a guy."

"I know you did." She looks away. "No, Karen, I don't think about going out. I mean, why should I? Nobody's gonna ask me."

"There's a guy who wants to."

"Who?"

"Charles Bronson."

Connie is again facing me, and it's hard to read her expression. Mostly it's blank, so I go on. "He's—"

"I know who Charles Bronson is," she says. "What makes you think I'd want to go out with him?"

The question surprises me. "He said that a few years back you were real nice to him. Helped him out of a jam."

"I've helped a lot of people who were in jams. That doesn't mean I want to date them."

Connie's voice has gone edgy, and it bothers me. "I thought you might like knowing that someone was interested."

"It depends a lot on who the someone is." She jumps up and stalks to the window. "I don't date guys who aren't cool."

"I didn't think you dated anyone," I say. "At least not these days."

"So that's it?" She whips around and glares at me. "Because I have AIDS, I should be grateful if anyone shows any interest in me at all."

"Because you have AIDS," I snap back, "you could at least be decent to anyone who wants to be your friend." I'm angry at how this whole conversation is going. "I mean that person is taking a risk. Being friends with someone who has AIDS doesn't exactly add to popularity."

"Is that what this is all about?"

"What?"

"Look, Karen, anytime you want to stop being friends, anytime it gets too rough for you, you can always leave. You've done that before."

I don't answer. I grab my books from the bed and storm out of her room, out of her house.

And now it's two weeks later, almost five o'clock in the afternoon. For over an hour I've been sitting outside the gym, waiting for cheerleading practice to end. If that doesn't happen soon, I'll have to go home. I've got dinner chores, two quizzes to study for, and a one-page essay to write for English.

Finally the doors to the gym swing open, and Rae comes out with a bunch of girls, laughing and talking. I feel a twinge of regret. When school opened more than two months ago, I was part of that group. I was cool. I belonged. But now? Now . . . Shutting off such thoughts, I call to Rae.

She sees me and comes over to the brick wall where I'm sitting. "What are you doing here?"

"I wanted to talk to you."

"Then let's go somewhere else. If Miss Barslow sees you, she'll probably kill you."

"Really mad, huh?"

"Really mad. But then most girls do let her know if they quit the cheerleading squad."

"I don't know if I've really quit."

"Oh, yes, you have. You stopped coming to practice. That means you've quit."

Rae's words bring me up short. I guess I have quit the cheerleading squad—and not in the most diplomatic way possible. I should have written, I should have at least spoken to Miss Barslow. But I didn't.

And now? Now I'm surprised at how little being a cheerleader—or not being a cheerleader—matters. Particularly when making the squad a little over a year ago was such a big deal.

"Come on." Rae's voice, hinting at impatience, brings me back to the present. She leads the way around to the side of the gym, where a three-tiered flight of stone steps leads down to the football field. There the team's about to finish practice. The players half-heartedly charge into each other, then break for laps. Beyond them are trees, bare of leaves, branches spindly against the late-afternoon sky.

"So what do you want to talk about?" she asks.

"The thing is," I begin, "I've made a couple of mistakes about who I was friends with and who I wasn't." I pause, realizing this is going to be harder than I expected. I can't just come out and say that hanging around with Connie was a bad idea. Rae'll think that Connie's contagious; she might even think that I've caught AIDS. It's probably best, I decide, to avoid the whole issue. "Now homecoming's this weekend, and I still have to go. I *am* on the court." I finish and extend my hands, palms up, in what I hope is a helpless gesture.

"And?" Rae says.

So much for her picking up the conversational ball. "I don't have a date," I say bluntly. "I thought if Todd hasn't asked anyone, the four of us could go together. You know, like always."

Rae gazes out over the football field and for a time seems to concentrate totally on the team. "Huh, huh, huh," the players chant as they run their final lap and head for the gym.

"Karen," she finally says, "it's not that easy."

"What's not?"

"Picking up again. Hanging out together."

"Sure it is. I can fix things with Todd. Shoot, I don't really need to fix things. He'll have what he wants. I'm not spending any time with Connie."

Rae's expression remains serious. She holds a stack of books in close to her chest. "It's not just Todd."

"Then what is it?"

"Parents. His and mine."

"What about them?" I ask, not understanding what she could be driving at.

"The thing is, Karen, they were pretty relieved a while back when you stopped hanging out with us. It solved a problem."

"Did it?" I hear the chill in my voice.

"Yes. You see, they were starting to say we shouldn't see you. They were a little paranoid about this AIDS thing. But then I guess everyone was." Rae tries a smile that doesn't work at all.

"And now?" I ask.

"Now it'd probably be the same. Karen, I hate to be saying this, but I have to. I can't start another hassle at home. There's already a bunch of stuff going down. My parents aren't happy with my grades. And they think Nick and I are getting way too close. You know how it is."

"Do I?" I stare at Rae, hoping for some sign that she's kidding. But I don't see one. She's dead serious.

I jam my hands into the pockets of my denim jacket, turn, and walk away. These past weeks, without Connie, without my old friends, have been pretty lonely. And now, I guess, things will stay that way.

chapter nine

~ "Nice," my mother says as I reach the bot tom of the stairs. She's in the living room, where a wing chair partly blocks her view, so she gets up and comes into the hallway for a closer look. "Very nice."

"Thanks." I knew my mother'd be pleased—at least with the way I look. Right after I made the homecoming court, she and I went shopping for my first formal, with all the accessories. So now I'm dressed in regulation homecoming court clothes—a long white dress, white gloves that extend halfway up my arms, and, of course, white shoes. A pink ribbon with a cameo is at my neck, and my hair is piled up in a really sophisticated style.

"When's Todd picking you up?" my mother asks.

I concentrate on my gloves. I smooth them. I make sure the seams lie straight on the outsides of my arms. All that keeps me from looking at my mother. "He's not," I say.

"You're meeting him there?" Her voice rings with surprise. "Oh, Karen." And moves into displeasure. "For an event this important, I should think—"

"I'm not meeting him there."

There's a silence.

"You're dating someone else?" my mother asks.

"No, Mother. I'm not." She knows that, I think.

"But the dance," she says. "You're all dressed up. Who are you going with?"

"No one. You did say I could use the car tonight, didn't you?"

"Yes, but I never thought—"

"Oh, Mom." I grab the car keys off the foyer table and dart out the door. I don't want to see my mother's concern; most of all I don't want to hear how inappropriate my behavior is. Why? Because it is, and I know it. I'm heading out to a dance, one of the biggest, most formal dances of the year, and I'm alone. Girls don't do that; they don't go to dances alone. They have a date, or they stay home. So why am I going? Because I have to. I'm on the court, and if I don't show up, there'll be rumors, probably about my health, like . . . Well, I don't even want to think about those rumors. I climb into the car and drive away.

The gym, when I enter, is dark, lit only by a mirror ball that throws pinpoints of light on the ceiling and walls. I stand at the edge of pushed-back bleachers, trying to figure out what to do. I suppose there are times in my life when I've felt more uncomfortable, but I can't think of when. All I see are couples. They're out on the floor dancing. They're entering the gymnasium, bringing with them a touch of the cold night. And they make me feel horribly alone.

I search out the stag line. Of course it's all male. Still I squint at it through the darkness, hoping I'll recognize someone I can talk to. But I don't. It's a collection of kids I don't know, kids who, like Charles Bronson, blend into the woodwork. I don't see Charles in the line, and I'm surprised.

At one end of the room is the refreshment table, and I wander off in that direction. Maybe I'll feel a little less awkward if I can balance a finger sandwich and a cup of punch. I take a long time selecting which sandwich I want and wait for fresh punch to be poured. Miss Ellis, faculty advisor to the SGA, bustles in from the kitchen, carrying a large tray filled with replacement sandwiches.

Seeing a way out of feeling so alone and useless, hurry over to her. "Miss Ellis?"

She glances up, her manner harried. "Oh, hello, Karen. My, but don't you look nice." She rests the tray on the table and wipes damp curls up from her forehead.

"And you look busy."

"Yes, I am. We all are." She nods at a crew of student workers.

"Need some more help?" I ask.

"From you? Mercy, no." Miss Ellis laughs, a gurgly sound that remains mostly in her throat.

"We can't have a member of the homecoming court carrying around sandwiches and punch."

"But I—"

"Karen, it's sweet of you to offer, but there's no way I'll take you up on it. You just go and find your date. Have fun." She puts the last of the sandwiches on a platter and scurries back into the kitchen.

Find my date? Have fun? Yeah. Sure. What I manage to find instead is a dark corner where at least I'm out of the way. Where *I* can blend into the woodwork. Like Charles Bronson. Like those other kids I never thought about until this fall. But I have my doubts. It's hard to feel blended in when you're dressed all in white and your hair—sophisticated style or not—is poking up eight inches above your head.

"Karen?" Mike Rowen comes up behind me. He has on a dark suit, and his hair is flattened down. I hardly recognize him. "You here alone?" he asks.

I hear the question and cringe. It embarrasses me, as if he's discovered some dirty secret that he's pulling out for the world to see. But embarrassed or not, I still have to answer. "Yep," I say, "I'm here alone." I smile broadly, showing that coming to the Homecoming Dance alone is something I've always wanted to do.

"No Todd?" he presses.

"No Todd."

"But I thought the two of you . . ."

"We haven't seen much of each other lately." I'm
surprised Mike hasn't heard. Our breakup was ho
gossip for a time.

"And you're here anyway." Mike shakes hi
head. "You've got guts, Karen. A lot more than
ever thought."

"I don't know," I say, still trying for a light
heartedness I don't feel. "You're here alone."

"Professional reasons." Mike taps his jacke
pocket where I assume his ever-present notebook i
kept. Then he smiles; his eyes begin to twinkle
"Now if you'd join—"

"No!" I break in quickly. But I realize that righ
now the thought of sitting in the newspaper office
few hours a day, concentrating on words and ideas
has a lot more appeal than the idea of dealing with
people. Or, more accurately, not dealing with peo
ple, since the people I used to deal with are n
longer around. Todd. Rae. And now Connie. The
thought makes me sad; my gee-it's-great-to-be
here-alone act crumples. "Oh, Mike, it's not guts,
hate being here by myself."

"Then why are you?"

"I figured if I didn't show up, everybody'd star
saying I was sick. Like Connie."

"I doubt it. I don't think anyone would have
noticed you weren't here."

"Really?" I gesture, drawing attention to my
dress.

"Oh, that's right. I'd forgotten you're on the court. Yeah, they probably would have noticed." His expression glides into amazement. "Are you going to do that alone, too?"

"Do I have a choice?"

"Yes."

For an instant Mike looks shy, and I understand what he's saying. I grin. Maybe Mike Rowen isn't the guy I would have chosen as my date for homecoming, but he's sure better than standing up on that stage in front of all these people alone.

And so we become a twosome. We dance. We drink punch and eat sandwiches. I nod knowingly when I have no idea what Mike is talking about. Occasionally he watches a couple on the dance floor or listens to what someone says and jots something down in his notebook.

Then, an hour and a half later, it's time for the ceremonies. Tony Phelps rounds up all the members of the homecoming court and makes sure we're standing near the stage. He takes the mike, reminds everyone—unnecessarily—that he's the SGA president, then introduces each member of the court. One by one, as our names are called, we climb up on the stage—with our dates—and take our places. I try not to notice that the applause following my name is only a smattering. I am, however, very glad Mike is at my side.

Finally, after all the court is on stage, after a few minutes of mindless chitchat, a few minutes of artificially created suspense, Tony announces that Elise Darlington is queen. I, along with the rest of the court, smile and clap. We're showing we're good sports, that we don't really care who won. Of course in my case it's not a matter of pretending to be a good sport. Not for one single second did I want to win.

Elise blinks back tears and seems genuinely surprised as the crown is placed on her head. It crosses my mind that maybe she isn't surprised at being chosen. Maybe the crown is heavier than it looks.

Then Tony has a few more words to say, and the event is over. Mike and I move back down onto the dance floor.

"Thanks," I say. "That would have been pretty miserable alone."

"It was nothing. Perhaps just a touch of fate. You know in literature it always seems—"

"Karen!" Connie, wearing a royal-blue satin dress with puffy sleeves and a scooped neckline, cuts around some dancers and catches up with Mike and me. Her hair is blond and flowing; makeup brings out the blue in her eyes, the peachy tones in her skin. I realize that, except for being pounds thinner, she looks pretty much the way she used to. And then I notice that close on her heels, carrying two cups of punch, is Charles Bronson. Whoa! I think. Looks like I missed some developments in the past few weeks.

"Hi, Connie," Mike says. "How ya doing?"